THE SANTINA CROWN

Royalty has never been so sc...

STOP THE PRESS—*crown prince i...*

The tabloid headlines…

When Crown Prince Alessandro of Santina proposes to
paparazzi favorite Allegra Jackson, the wedding promises to
be the social event of the decade.

Outrageous headlines guaranteed!

The salacious gossip…

Harlequin Presents invites you to rub shoulders with royalty,
sheikhs and glamorous socialites. Step into the decadent
playground of the world's rich and famous, where
*one thing is for sure—
royalty has never been so scandalous!*

Beginning May 2012

THE PRICE OF ROYAL DUTY—Penny Jordan

THE SHEIKH'S HEIR—Sharon Kendrick

SANTINA'S SCANDALOUS PRINCESS—Kate Hewitt

THE MAN BEHIND THE SCARS—Caitlin Crews

DEFYING THE PRINCE—Sarah Morgan

PRINCESS FROM THE SHADOWS—Maisey Yates

THE GIRL NOBODY WANTED—Lynn Raye Harris

PLAYING THE ROYAL GAME—Carol Marinelli

"It's your lucky day, Lord Pembroke," she confided, leaning in closer and tapping her champagne flute against his chest.

He felt it like a caress. She looked at him, and something dark moved across her pretty face, something too like grief, there and then gone in her expressive eyes. "I happen to be interviewing candidates for the position of wealthy husband, and you fit the bill."

And suddenly it all made sense.

This, Rafe thought, everything going very still inside him, he understood perfectly.

Caitlin Crews

THE MAN BEHIND THE SCARS

HARLEQUIN®
entertain, enrich, inspire™

Recycling programs
for this product may
not exist in your area.

ISBN-13: 978-0-373-13084-9

THE MAN BEHIND THE SCARS

Copyright © 2012 by Harlequin Books S.A.

Special thanks and acknowledgment are given to Caitlin Crews for her contribution to The Santina Crown series.

All about the author...
Caitlin Crews

CAITLIN CREWS discovered her first romance novel at the age of twelve. It involved swashbuckling pirates, grand adventures, a heroine with rustling skirts and a mind of her own, and a seriously mouthwatering and masterful hero. The book (the title of which remains lost in the mists of time) made a serious impression. Caitlin was immediately smitten with romances and romance heroes, to the detriment of her middle school social life. And so began her lifelong love affair with romance novels, many of which she insists on keeping near her at all times.

Caitlin has made her home in places as far-flung as York, England, and Atlanta, Georgia. She was raised near New York City and fell in love with London on her first visit when she was a teenager. She has backpacked in Zimbabwe, been on safari in Botswana and visited tiny villages in Namibia. She has, while visiting each place in question, declared her intention to live in Prague, Dublin, Paris, Athens, Nice, the Greek Islands, Rome, Venice and/or any of the Hawaiian islands. Writing about exotic places seems like the next best thing to moving there.

She currently lives in California, with her animator/comic-book-artist husband and their menagerie of ridiculous animals.

Other titles by Caitlin Crews available in eBook:

Harlequin Presents®

To Josh Moon, who explained construction to me in very detailed terms that he will be sure I didn't use at all in this book. But I did!

CHAPTER ONE

IT WAS one thing to boldly decide that you were going to capture a rich husband to save you from your life, and more to the point from the desperate financial situation you'd discovered you were in through no fault of your own, Angel Tilson thought a bit wildly as she stared around the glittering ballroom, but quite another thing to *do* it.

She didn't know what her problem was. She was standing knee-deep in a sea of wealthy, titled people. Everywhere she looked she saw money, nobility and actual royalty, filling the sparkling ballroom of the Palazzo Santina and threatening to outshine the massive chandeliers that hung dramatically overhead. She could *feel* the wealth saturating the very air, like an exclusive scent.

The whole island seemed to be bursting at the seams with this prince, that sheikh and any number of flash European nobles, their ancient titles and inherited ranks hanging from their elegant limbs like the kind of fine accessories Angel herself could never afford. It was the first time in Angel's twenty-eight years that she'd ever found herself in a room—a palace ballroom, to be sure, but it was still, technically, a room—with a selection of princes. As in, *princes plural*.

She should have been overjoyed. She told herself she was. She'd come all the way from her questionable neighborhood in London to beautiful Santina, this little jewel of an island kingdom in the Mediterranean, in order to personally celebrate her favorite stepsister's surprising engagement to a real, live prince. And she was happy for Allegra and her lovely Prince Alessandro—of course she was. Thrilled, in fact. But if sweet, sensible Allegra could bag herself the Crown Prince of Santina, Angel didn't see why she couldn't find herself a wealthy husband of her own here in this prosperous, red-roofed little island paradise, where rich men seemed to be as thick on the ground as Mediterranean weeds.

He didn't even have to be royal, she thought generously, eyeing the assorted male plumage before her from her position near one of the grand pillars that lined the great room—all Angel needed was a nice, big, healthy bank account.

She wanted to pretend it was all a game—but it wasn't. Not to put too fine a point on it, but she was desperate.

She felt herself frown then, and made a conscious effort to smooth her expression away into something more enticing. Or at least something vaguely pleasant. Scowling was hardly likely to appeal to anyone, much less inspire sudden marriage proposals from the sort of men who could buy all the smiles they liked, the way common folk like Angel bought milk and eggs.

"You can just as easily smile as frown, love," her mother had always said in that low, purring way of hers, usually punctuated with one of Chantelle's trademark sexy smirks or bawdy laughs. That and "why not marry a rich one if you must marry one at all" constituted the bulk of the maternal advice Chantelle—never *Mum*, always *Chantelle*, no age ever mentioned in public, thank you—had offered. But thinking about her conniving, thoughtless mother did not help. Not now, while she was standing knee-deep in another one of Chantelle's messes.

Hurt and fury and incomprehension boiled inside of her all over again as she thought of the fifty thousand quid her mother had run up on a credit card she'd "accidentally" taken out in Angel's name. Angel had discovered the horrifying bill on her doormat one day, so seemingly innocuous at a casual glance that she'd almost thrown it in the bin. She'd had to sit down, she'd been so dizzy, staring at the statement in her hand until it made, if not sense in the usual meaning of the term, a certain sickening kind of *Chantelle* sense.

Once she'd got past the initial shock, she'd known at once that her mother was the culprit—that it wasn't some kind of mistake. She'd hated that she'd known, and she'd hated the nausea that went with that knowing, but she'd known even so. It was not the first time Chantelle had "borrowed" money from Angel, nor even the first "accident", but it was the first time she'd let herself get *this* carried away.

"I've just received a shocking bill from a credit card account I never opened," she'd snapped down the phone when her mother had answered in her usual breezy, careless manner, as if all was right with her world. Which, at fifty thousand pounds the richer, perhaps it was.

"Right," Chantelle had drawled out, in that slightly shocked way of hers that told Angel that, as usual, her mother had not thought through to the consequences of her actions. Had she ever? Would she ever? "I've been meaning to talk to you about that, love," Chantelle had murmured. "You won't want to ruin Allegra's do this weekend with this sort of unpleasantness, of course, but we'll have loads of time afterward to—"

Angel had simply ended the call with a violent jerk of

her hand, unable to speak for fear that she would scream herself hoarse. And then cry like the child she'd never really been, not when she'd had to play the adult to Chantelle's excesses from such a young age—and she never cried. Never. Not over Chantelle's innumerable deficiencies as a mother and a human being. Not for a single reason that she could recall. What problem did tears ever solve?

Fifty thousand, she thought now, standing in the middle of the dazzling ballroom, but it didn't feel real. Not the fairy-tale beauty and elegance of the palace around her, and not that stunning number either. The sickening enormity of that sum of money rolled through Angel like thunder, low and long, and she wasn't sure, for a moment, if she could breathe through the sheer panic that followed in its wake, making her skin feel clammy and her breath shallow. *Fifty thousand pounds.*

Neither she nor Chantelle had a hope in hell of paying off a sum that large. In what universe? Chantelle's single claim to fame was her marriage to beloved ex-footballer and regular subject of tabloid speculation and gossip Bobby Jackson. It had resulted in Angel's wild-child half sister, the sometime pop idol, Izzy, who Angel did not pretend to understand, and very little else. Aside from notoriety, of course. Chantelle had been a market stall owner before she'd set out to net herself one of England's favorite sons. No one had ever let her forget it. Not that Chantelle seemed to care—she got to bask in Bobby's reflected glory, didn't she?

Angel had learned better than to inquire after the state of Bobby and Chantelle's deeply cynical union a long, long time ago, lest she be subject to another lecture from her relentless social climber of a mother on how marriage, if done correctly and to a minor celebrity like big-spending and large-living Bobby, was simple common sense and good business. Angel shuddered now, trying to imagine what it was like to remain married to a man that *everyone in the whole of England* knew was still sleeping with his ex-wife, Julie. If not many others besides. How could Chantelle be so proud of her marriage when every tabloid in the UK knew the shameful state of it? Angel didn't know.

What she did know was that there were certainly no heretofore undiscovered stashes of pounds sterling lying about Bobby's house in Hertfordshire or the flat in Knightsbridge Chantelle preferred, or Chantelle wouldn't have had to "borrow" from her own daughter in the first place, would she? The truth was, Angel suspected that Bobby had cut Chantelle off from his purse strings long ago. Or had emptied out that purse all by himself, with all of his good-natured if shortsighted ways.

Angel couldn't seem to fight off the sadness that moved through her then as she thought—not for the first time— what her life might have been like if Chantelle had been a normal sort of mother. If Chantelle had cared about someone other than herself. Not that Angel could complain. Not really. She'd always been treated well enough by Bobby's rowdy brood of children from his various wives and lovers—even by Julie, if she was honest—and the truth was that carelessly genial Bobby was the only father she'd ever known. Angel's real, biological father had done a runner the moment seventeen-year-old Chantelle had told him she was pregnant. Angel had always been grateful for the way the Jackson clan—especially Bobby—had included her. They'd tried, and that was more than others might have done. But at the end of the day she wasn't a Jackson like the rest of them, was she?

Angel had always been far too aware of that crucial distinction. She'd always felt that boundary line, invisible but impossible to ignore, marking the difference between all

of them, and her. She'd always been on the outside looking in, no matter how many Christmases she spent with
them, pretending. The Jacksons were the only family she
had, but that didn't make them *hers*. All she had, for her
sins, was Chantelle.

Angel wished, not for the first time, that she'd gone on
to university. That she'd dedicated herself to an education,
a career—*something.* But she'd been so very pretty at sixteen, blessed with her mother's infamous blagging skills
and the body to back them up. She'd been confident that
she could make her own way in the world, and she had, one
way or another. She'd talked her way into more jobs than
she could count since then, none of them long-lasting, but
she'd always told herself that that was how she liked it. No
ties. Nothing that could hold her back should she need to
move on. She'd been muse and model to a fashion designer,
had run her own retail shop for a year or two, and could
usually pick up some kind of modeling job or another in a
pinch. It was always a struggle, but she paid her rent and
her bills, and often had a little bit left over, as well.

Not fifty thousand quid, of course. Not anything even
remotely close to that.

Her stomach heaved, and she pressed her fist against her
belly as if that would settle it, by force. By her will alone.
What was she supposed to do? Declare bankruptcy? Have
her mother arrested for identity fraud? However angry she
was, however hurt, *again,* she couldn't quite see taking
either route. One was humiliating and unfair. The other
was unthinkable.

Right, she thought then, her usual cool and practical
nature taking over at last, shoving the unfamiliar lash-
ings of self-pity aside. *Enough whingeing, Angel. This is
a once-in-a-lifetime opportunity tonight. Pull yourself together and use it!*

Angel helped herself to a flute of champagne from a passing waiter, took a restorative sip and squared her shoulders. She decided to ignore the faint trembling in her hands. She was Angel Tilson. She was tough—she'd had to be, the whole of her life. She did not break at the first sign of adversity—or even at fifty thousand pounds' worth of signs. She did not recognize defeat. As Bobby had always said—while throwing the odd drink down his throat, but the sentiment was the same regardless—*defeat* was nothing more than an *opportunity* to succeed the next time. And the glorious thing about having no options was that she had absolutely no choice but to succeed.

"So," she murmured to herself, fiercely, "I bloody well will."

Her reasons for going ahead and playing this game might have been desperate, but that didn't change the fact that it was a game she was very good at playing. How could she not be, she thought with something like dark humor. It was in her genes.

She ran her free hand over the curve of her hip, making sure her dress was in place, sticking like glue to the tight, toned curves she'd inherited directly from her mother. She could not quite bring herself to be grateful to Chantelle for that little gift. Not quite. Not tonight. The dress was strapless, short and black as sin—and pretended to be decorous while instead showing off every mouthwatering inch of what was, she knew, her only weapon and greatest asset. Her body.

Nearby, a gaunt-faced older man with centuries of breeding stamped into his sunken bones and his so-proper-it-hurt wife stared at her as if she'd committed some hideous breach of etiquette right there in front of them. Anything was possible, of course, but Angel knew she'd successfully kept a low profile here at Allegra's party—so outside her realm of experience was it to find herself in a *palace*. The well-bred couple averted their eyes in apparent horror, and Angel bit back a laugh.

She'd leave the truly appalling behavior to the rest of the Jackson family, as she suspected her half sister and stepsiblings, all seven gathered together under this much-too-elegant roof, were more than up to the task. It was, in fact, a Jackson family tradition to stir up scandal wherever they went.

Her half sister, Izzy, had recently been involved in a highly publicized engagement that had ended so dramatically and so openly—at the altar, no less, flashbulbs popping—that Angel had cynically assumed it was all part of her younger sister's increasingly desperate bid for attention from the less and less interested press. Izzy was as bad as their mother, who was no doubt also in this huge crowd somewhere right now, flinging her mane of blonde hair about like a woman half her age, inevitably dressed in something scandalous and up to who knew what. They could even be up to their usual mischief *together*—a prospect Angel couldn't bear to think about any further.

She, on the other hand, had to be just well-behaved enough to catch the right sort of eye—and just badly behaved enough to make sure that eye didn't stray. When the gaunt older man snuck an appreciative second look at her figure behind his wife's stiff and scandalized back, Angel smiled in satisfaction. The game was on.

She prowled around the edge of the great gala event, fortified with another glass of the remarkably good champagne, scanning the party for any possibilities. After some consideration and a long look at an obviously wealthy-looking sort with an unfortunate nose that could, in a pinch, double as a bridge over the English Channel, she admitted that she was, regrettably, not *that* desperate. Not yet.

Looking around, she also automatically excluded any men with women already hanging off of them, or even standing too close to them, as she didn't have the time or inclination to compete, and anyway, she wasn't at all interested in someone *else's* husband.

She might have descended to following in her mother's footsteps and becoming a shameless gold digger, she thought piously, but she did have *some* standards.

She took care to avoid any of the Jackson family, Chantelle and Izzy included—or perhaps especially—as she moved through the crowd. Those she was particularly close to—like the bride-to-be Allegra herself or Ben, the eldest Jackson sibling and as close to a big brother as Angel was likely to get—she was determined to avoid at all costs. She couldn't handle any sort of show of concern, not from the people she actually considered near enough to family. She didn't want either of them to ask her how she was doing, because she might accidentally let the awful truth slip out in all its ugliness, and that would hardly put her in the right frame of mind to catch a husband, would it?

Not that she had any idea what frame of mind that was meant to be, she thought wryly, slipping behind another pillar to avoid a tight scrum of what, to her untrained eye, looked like a pack of highly disapproving priests. Or possibly bankers.

And that was when she saw him.

He was lurking—there was no better word for it—almost in the shadows of the next pillar, all by himself, presenting Angel with a view of his commanding profile. He was…magnificent. That was also the best word for it. For him. She paused for a moment, letting her eyes travel all over him. His shoulders were wide and strong, and his torso looked like packed steel beneath a suit that should have been elegant, but on his lean, rugged frame was instead…something else. Something that whispered of great power, ruthlessly and not altogether seamlessly contained. He stood with his feet apart and his hands thrust into the pockets of his trousers, and she got the impression that there was something almost belligerent in that stance, something profoundly dangerous.

Every hair on her body seemed to stand on end.

There was just something about him, Angel thought unsteadily as another kind of thunder seemed to roll through her then, making her breath seem harder to catch than it should have been. She couldn't seem to look away. Maybe it was his thick dark hair, too long to be strictly correct and at distinct and intriguing odds with the conservative suit he wore. Maybe it was the brooding, considering way he looked out over the ballroom, as if he saw nothing at all to catch his interest, nothing to combat whatever it was he carried inside of him, like a deep shadow within yet almost visible to the naked eye. Maybe it was that lean jaw, and the grim mouth that Angel suddenly felt was some kind of challenge, though she couldn't have said why.

Whatever else this man was, she thought then, anticipation and adrenaline coursing through her, making her whole body seem to hum into alertness, he was a candidate. She moved toward him, pleased to note that the closer she got, the more impressive he was. There was a certain watchful stillness to him that she felt like an echo beneath her ribs. She wasn't at all surprised when he turned his head to pin her with a cold, dark stare while she was still several feet away—and she got the sudden and distinct impression that he'd sensed her approach from the start, from the moment she'd laid eyes on him. As if he was preternaturally *aware* of everything that happened around him.

For a moment, she saw nothing but that stare. Cold gray eyes, the most remote she'd ever seen, and darker than anyone's ought to be. He seemed to see into her, through her, as if she was entirely transparent. As if she was made of some insubstantial bit of glass. As if he could read her desperation, her dreams, her plans and her flimsy hopes, in a single, searing glance. She *felt* it, him, everywhere.

She blinked—and then she saw his scars.

A wide, devastating set of once angry, now simply brutal scars swiped across the whole left side of his face, raking him from temple to chin, sparing his eye but ravaging the rest of the side of his face and carrying on to loop under his hard, masculine chin. She sucked in a shocked breath, but she didn't stop walking. She couldn't, somehow, as if he compelled her. As if he had already pulled her in and she was only bowing to the inevitable.

What a shame, she thought, because the part of his face not damaged by the scars was undeniably handsome. She could see the thrust of his cheekbones, that tough line of his jaw. And that untouched mouth, entirely too hard and male, with that stamp of darkness—but inarguably attractive. More than attractive. As magnetic, somehow, as it was grim.

But there was another part of her—the practical part, she told herself, forged at her callous and cold mother's knee—that whispered, *The scars make it all the better.* As if he was some kind of an easy target because of them. As if they made him as desperate as she was.

She hated herself for thinking it. Deeply and profoundly. Like acid in her veins. But she kept walking.

His eyes grew colder the closer she came, and were very nearly glacial and intimidatingly stern when she came to a stop in front of him. He held himself silent and still, with the thrust and heft of his clearly evident power all but *glowing* beneath what had to be superb self-control. She told herself it was only nerves that made her mouth so dry, and sipped at her champagne to wet it. And to brace herself.

The woman in her liked that he was an inch or so taller than she was in her wicked four-inch heels. And the mercenary part of her liked the fact that he practically exuded wealth and consequence. He might as well wave it like a banner over his dark head. It was glaringly obvious in the elegant simplicity of everything he wore—all of it boasting the kind of stark, simple lines that came only with exorbitant price tags from the foremost ateliers. She knew. She'd worn that sort of clothing when she'd modeled—the kind of high couture that she could never have dreamed of buying herself. But she'd studied it all from an envious distance. She knew it when she saw it.

"You appear to be lost," he said, in a low, stirring sort of voice, for all that it was noticeably unfriendly. Or anyway, remote as his gaze. As uninviting. Luckily, Angel was not easily fazed. "The party is behind you."

His voice seemed to curl into her, around her, like the touch of a hard, calloused hand. It was also very, very posh. Angel smiled, and then tilted her head slightly to one side, considering him. If possible, his dark eyes grew even colder than before, the line of his mouth grimmer.

She knew then, with a sudden flash of something too like foreboding for her peace of mind, that nothing about this man would ever be *easy,* whether he was target—a candidate for this game of hers—or not. And more, perhaps even more importantly, that a man like this was unlikely to be impressed with a woman like her. But she shook that off almost as soon as she thought it. It was the challenge of it, she decided in that moment. She wasn't one to back down. She preferred to jump in feet first, and sort it all out later. She might have cooked up this make-your-own-fairy-tale plan in a wild panic on her flight across Europe, but that didn't mean it wasn't a good one. There was surely no point in changing her plan or even her wicked ways now. No point in false advertising, either. She was who she was, take it or leave it.

Most left it, of course, or ran up exorbitant debts in her name, but she told herself she was better for the things she'd lived through. Stronger anyway. Tougher.

She didn't know why she suspected that, with this man, she'd have to be. Or why that suspicion didn't send her running for the pretty green hills she'd seen as her plane came in to land on this magical little island.

"What happened to your face?" she asked, simple and direct, and waited to see what he'd do.

Rafe McFarland, who loathed the fact that he was currently dressed in fine and uncomfortable clothes for the express purpose of trumpeting his eminence as the Eighth Earl of Pembroke to all of his royal Santina cousins, as duty demanded, stared at the woman before him in the closest he'd come to shock in a long, long time.

He could not have heard her correctly.

But her perfectly arched eyebrows rose inquiringly over her sky-blue eyes, making her remarkably pretty face seem clever, and she regarded him with the kind of amused patience that suggested he had, in fact, heard her perfectly.

Rafe was well-used to women like this one catching sight of him from afar and heading toward him with that swing in their hips and that purpose in their eyes. He knew exactly how irresistible he'd once been to women—he had only to look at the remnants of what he'd once taken for granted in the mirror. He knew the whole, sad dance by heart. They advanced on him, delicious curves poured into dresses like the one this woman wore, that made her body look like a fantasy come to life—until he showed them the whole of his face.

Which he always did. Deliberately. Even cruelly.

It was, he knew all too well, a face that no one could bear to look at for long, least of all himself. It was the face of a monster all dressed up in a five-thousand-pound bespoke Italian suit, and Rafe lived with the bitter knowledge that the scars were not the half of it—not compared to the monster within. He took his terrible face out into public less and less these days, because he found the dance more and more difficult to bear with anything approaching equanimity. It always ended the same way. The more polite ones abruptly fixed their attention to a point just beyond him and walked on by, never sparing him another glance. The less polite gasped in horror as if they'd seen the very devil himself and then turned back around in a hurry. He had seen it all a hundred times. He couldn't even say the specific reactions bothered him anymore. He told himself they were, at the very least, honest. The sad truth was that he was grateful, on some level, for the scars that so helpfully advertised how deeply unsuited he was to human interaction of any kind. Better they should all be warned off in advance.

This woman, however, in her tiny black dress that licked over her tight, perfect curves, with her short and choppy blonde hair that seemed as bold and demanding as her sharp, too-clear blue eyes, had kept right on coming—even after he'd presented her with his face. With a full view of the scars that marked him as the monster he'd always known he was, since long before he'd had to wear the evidence on his face.

And then she'd actually asked him a direct question about those scars.

In all the years since his injury, this had never happened.

Which alone would have made it interesting. The fact that she was so beautiful it made him ache in ways he'd thought he never would again—well, that was just an added bonus.

"No one ever asks me that," he heard himself say, almost as if he was used to conversations with strangers. Or anyone he did not employ. "Certainly not directly. It is the elephant in the room. Or perhaps the Elephant Man in the room, to be more precise."

If possible, she looked even more closely at his scars, tracing the sweep of them with her bright blue gaze. Rafe hardly looked at them himself anymore, except to note that they remained right where he'd last seen them, no longer red and furious, perhaps, but certainly nothing like unnoticeable either. They did not blend. They did not, as a wildly optimistic plastic surgeon had once suggested they might, fade. Not enough to matter. And anyway, he preferred them to stay right where they were. There was less possibility of confusion if he wore the truth about himself right there on his face. He didn't know how he felt about this strange woman looking so intently at them, *really* looking at them, but he didn't do anything to stop her, and eventually her clever eyes moved back to his.

A kind of thunderclap reverberated through him. It took a moment to realize it was pure desire, punching into his gut.

"It's only a bit of scarring," she replied, that same smile on her mouth, her tone light. Airy. Teasing him, he realized in some kind of amazement. She was actually *teasing* him. "You're hardly the Phantom of the Opera, are you?"

Rafe couldn't remember the last time he'd smiled at a society event, even before he'd had this face of his to bear stoically and pretend didn't bother him. He couldn't remember the last time he'd smiled at all, come to that. But something closer to a smile than he'd felt in ages threatened the corners of his mouth, and more surprising than that, for a moment he considered giving in to it.

"I was in the army," he said. He watched her absorb that with a small nod and a narrowing of her lovely eyes, as if she was fitting him into some category in her head. He wondered which one. Then he wondered why on earth he should care. "There was an ambush and an explosion."

He hated himself for that—for such a stripped-down description of something that should never be explained away in an easy little sentence. As if two throwaway words did any justice to the horror, the pain. The sudden bright light, the deafening noise. His friends, gone in an instant if they had been lucky. Others, much less lucky. And Rafe, the least lucky of all, with his long, nightmare-ridden, scarred agony of survival.

It was no wonder he never looked in the mirror anymore. There were too many ghosts.

He didn't intend to give her any further details, so he should not have felt slightly disappointed that she didn't ask. But she also hadn't turned away, and he found that contrary to all of his usual instincts where beautiful women at tedious, drink-sodden society events were concerned, however few he'd attended in recent years, he didn't want her to.

"I'm Angel Tilson," she said, and offered him her hand, still smiling, as easily as if she spoke to monsters every day and found it—him—completely unremarkable. But then, he reminded himself sharply, she could only see the surface. She had no idea what lurked beneath. "Stepsister to Allegra, the beautiful bride-to-be."

Angel, he repeated in his head, in a manner he might have found appallingly close to sentimental had she not been standing there in front of him, that teasing smile still crooking her lips, her blue eyes daring him. *Daring him.*

He had the strangest sensation then—as if, despite ev-

erything, he might just be alive after all, just like every-
body else. And that same intense desire seemed to move
through him then, setting him on fire.

"Rafe McFarland," he said, and then, more formally,
"Lord Pembroke. Distant cousin to the Santinas, through
some exalted ancestor or another."

He took her hand and, obeying an urge he did not care
to examine and could not quite understand, lifted it to
his lips. Something arced between them when their skin
met, his mouth against the soft back of her hand, something white-hot and wild, and for a moment it was as if the
Palazzo Santina fell away, as if there was no well-blooded
crowd playing the usual drunken games all around them,
no strains of soothing music wafting through the air, nothing at all but *this*.

Heat. Light. Sex.

Impossible, Rafe thought abruptly.

He let go, because that was the exact opposite of what he
wanted to do. Her smile seemed brighter than the gleaming chandeliers high above them, and he couldn't seem to
look away. She was much too pretty to be looking at him
like this, as if he was the man he should have been. The
man he'd pretended to be, before the accident.

As if he wasn't ruined.

Perhaps, he thought darkly, she was blind.

"Lord Pembroke," she repeated, as if she was tasting the
title with her lush little mouth. He felt a flash of appreciation for the earldom in an area he had never before associated with it. "What does that mean, exactly? Besides the
fancy title and all the forelock tugging I assume goes with
it? A stately home and an Oxbridge education, with guest
appearances in *Tatler* to whet the appetite of the common-
ers from time to time?"

He liked her. It was revolutionary, but there it was. He hardly knew what to make of it.

"It means I am an earl," he said, with rather too much pompous emphasis, he thought, suddenly deeply tired of himself. But it was who he was. It had been all that he was for longer than he cared to admit, even to himself, even before he'd inherited the title—when he'd had only the sense of its import and the abiding respect for it that his wretched older brother had sorely lacked. He shook off the ghost of Oliver, Seventh Earl of Pembroke and drunken disgrace to the title. He wished he could shake off Oliver's legacy of debts and disasters, cruelty and sheer viciousness, as easily. "I have responsibilities, and little time for the tabloids, I'm afraid."

"That would be a yes then, on the grand old estate and Oxbridge and all the rest," Angel said, still teasing him, not appearing in the least bit cowed by his dark tone. "And I suppose you're also filthy rich. Doesn't that usually go hand in hand with nobility? A bit of compensation for the heavy load of the peerage and generations of privilege and so on?"

He didn't deny it, and she laughed as if he'd said something delightful. He almost felt as if he had.

"I don't know about *filthy* rich." He considered. He wondered why he didn't find this entire topic distasteful, as he should. As he imagined he would under any other circumstances. But he didn't, and he knew the reason he didn't was looking at him with far too blue and direct a gaze. He wanted to touch her. He wanted to see if she was real. Among, he admitted in some grudging surprise, other things. "But there are several centuries' worth of grime, I'd say. Certainly dirty enough for anyone."

She laughed again, and he became a stranger to himself in that moment, as he actually contemplated joining in. *Impossible,* he thought again.

"It's your lucky day, Lord Pembroke," she confided, leaning in closer and tapping her champagne flute against his chest. He felt it like a caress. She looked at him, and something dark moved across her pretty face, something too like grief there and then gone in her expressive eyes. "I happen to be interviewing candidates for the position of wealthy husband, and you fit the bill."

And suddenly it all made sense.

This, Rafe thought, everything going very still inside of him, he understood perfectly.

CHAPTER TWO

"You want to marry into money," he said, his voice cold, as if she had confirmed something he'd already suspected about her.

Angel wished she could tell what he thought of that—or even of her unapologetic way of presenting it. But his dark expression was impossible to read, and she wondered if her stomach could twist any further, and harder, and if it did…would she simply be sick? Right here?

She couldn't believe she'd actually said that. So baldly. So brashly.

But this was the plan. The only one she had, and so what if it had sounded much better in her head? She had no choice but to follow it—because no matter how humiliating this moment was and no matter how much she hated herself and would, she thought, loathe herself forevermore, she could not currently pay her mother's debts. There was no way. So this was what she'd come to. This terrible game while this affecting, compelling man only looked at her, his gray eyes cold and stern, and she wanted to be someone else—anyone else—more than she'd ever wanted anything.

Good luck with that, she thought darkly, and kept going.

"I do," she said, and shoved aside the part of her that wanted to drown in the shame, the tidal wave of embarrassment. That kind of second-guessing was for other women, perhaps, but not for her.

"Bold as brass, you are," her mother had always said, pretending to compliment Angel when she had really meant to compliment herself, because Angel so greatly resembled her. *And now more than ever,* Angel thought viciously.

She waved her champagne glass languidly, indicating the ballroom all around them and the party that carried on, all appropriate voices and hushed royal splendor behind them, though she never dropped his gaze. "I will."

Angel watched some kind of quiet storm move through his dark gray eyes then, and discovered she was barely breathing. But she was still smiling, damn it. She was afraid that if she stopped, she might have to investigate the self-loathing and the sheer, dizzying whirl of something too close to terror beneath it. This man was not at all what she'd imagined when she'd comforted herself with visions of *a wealthy husband to solve all my problems, just like Allegra* on the plane ride to Santina. Just as she hadn't imagined that she would feel something like that jolting, electric thrill that had sizzled through her when he'd touched her. What was *that?*

"Ah," he said, his voice even lower than before, but still with that same effect on her. And, she thought, faintly condemning. Or perhaps she was only hearing the echo of her own, now-buried shame. "And why do you need a wealthy husband?"

"I thought about simply asking for charitable donations," Angel said with a little smirk. He waited. She shrugged expansively. "A better question is, who *doesn't* need a wealthy husband? Given the choice."

"You appear to be making the choice yourself, rather than waiting for it to be presented to you," Rafe said in that dry way of his that seemed to move through her like heat. "Very enterprising."

"I'm extremely practical," she told him, as if confiding in him. As if his words had been in any way approving.

"You'd have to be," he agreed, "if you mean to choose a spouse in so cold and calculating a manner."

"Is that meant to chastise me?" she asked lightly, as if she hardly noticed one way or the other. As if it would be nothing to her if, in fact, he did mean to do exactly that. A lie, she realized in some surprise—but she shrugged carelessly anyway. "I know what I want and am prepared to go after it. I believe that when a man exhibits this kind of single-minded determination, whole nations rise up and applaud his focus and drive. Sometimes grateful kings bestow earldoms upon such men, if I remember my history." She smiled, though it was a bit more pointed than was strictly necessary. "Though it's been a while."

His grim, hard mouth entertained the faintest ghost of what she told herself was a smile. Or could have been, had he allowed it. His dark eyes gleamed. In appreciation, she was sure of it.

"You are a very beautiful woman," he said, and the way he said it, so matter-of-factly and without the slightest whiff of flattery, prevented her from the folly of imagining it was a compliment. "You are obviously well aware of it, as you've dressed to showcase and emphasize your many charms. A man would have to be dead to fail to notice that you are quite spectacular."

"Thank you," she said, her own voice dry this time. "This must be what it feels like to be a show horse. Or so I assume. There weren't too many thoroughbreds littered about the streets of Brixton the last time I left my flat."

Her flat was smack in a scruffy bit of Brixton, south London, that was considered *edgy* and *unpretentious,* she

knew, having read that exact claim in the guidebooks—
which she imagined was another way of saying *a bit dodgy*.
Still, it was the home she'd carved out for herself—the only
one that had ever really been hers.

"It seems to me you could simply captivate the man of
your choosing in the usual way, without having to make
crass pronouncements about marrying for money." His
dark eyebrow rose then, challenging and faintly wicked.
It was the left one, sliced through with a scar, making him
seem vaguely menacing, and entirely too lofty, all at once.
But not, she noted after a moment, menacing in a way that
actually frightened her, as perhaps it should have done. "I
think you'll find that your sort of beauty, used with a certain clarity of purpose, is the currency upon which many
marriages rest—though the participants do not generally
speak of it."

This time, there was no pretending he wasn't chastis-
ing her. He was—in that excruciatingly polite, excessively
wordy aristocratic way, complete with the expected back-
handed compliment to remind her of her place. Her *sort of
beauty*. How patronizing. Angel rolled her eyes.

"I am many things, *my lord*," she said, unable to keep
the faint note of mockery from her voice as she addressed
him formally, but equally unable to keep that smile from
her face, as if she was, somehow, enjoying this. Was she?
Surely not. "Crass, for example. As common as muck, certainly. But never a liar."

She didn't understand why she couldn't seem to look
away from this man, and his ravaged, ruined face. Why
she kept forgetting to look at the scars and found herself
lost in the remote coldness of his gaze instead. Why the
ballroom around them seemed like a bright blur, and he
was the only thing in focus. The only thing at all.

"So what are your specifications then?" he asked after

a stretch of time, highly charged and breathless, that could have been a moment or an hour. "For the perfect husband?"

"He must be very, very wealthy, and happy to share it," Angel said at once. "That's the main thing, and is, of course, nonnegotiable." She bit her lip as if ticking off items in a list in her head. "And it would be lovely if he were good-looking, too."

"A pity," he said softly, that menace in his tone again, and written across his destroyed face, though his eyes seemed darker then, and his gaze sharper. Her stomach clenched in reaction. "You're wasting your time with me. Or have you blocked out my scars from the sheer horror of looking at them too long?"

"It was the talk of your grimy, dirty money, of course," she replied at once, finding her way back into the light, teasing tone she'd been using so carelessly before. Because she had the sudden sense that what she said now could make all the difference, somehow. That it mattered. She felt it deep in her gut. "I haven't seen straight since you mentioned it. And depending on how much we're talking about, I may never see straight again."

"I am remarkably rich," he said, that deep, aristocratic voice a posh drawl now, pure male confidence in every syllable. It was a dare, she thought, though she could not have said, looking at that deliberately expressionless, dangerous face of his, why she thought so.

"Is that an offer?" she asked, flirting with him. With this whole crazy idea that seemed less and less impossible by the second. A fairy tale by design, on demand. Why not? She was already standing in a palace, wasn't she?

Again, that suggestion of a smile that, still, was not one.

"Why do you need money so badly that you would marry a stranger for it rather than simply finding yourself a well-paying career?" His eyes moved over her face as if searching for her intentions. As if he could read them there, if he looked hard enough. She feared he could. That he could see her cobbled-together history of temporary gigs that led nowhere, built nothing and depended entirely on her looks. What *career* was there for the likes of her? "What do you imagine you'll do with it?"

"Count the great big piles of it," she retorted easily, flippantly, as if she hadn't a single serious thought in her head. "Naturally. Isn't that what rich people do?"

"Only part of the time," he said. Was that a joke? It was interesting how very much she wanted it to be. "But it is a finite exercise."

"How finite?" she asked, a smile tugging at her lips. She tilted her head slightly to one side. "Five years? Ten?"

"Thirty at most," he said gravely, but she saw the gleam in those gunmetal-gray depths, and imagined this was his version of laughing. She felt an answering sort of tightness in her chest. As if they were connected, or ought to be. "What will you do with the rest of your time?"

She considered him for a moment, and then decided she might as well go for it. *No false advertising,* she reminded herself. *Bold as brass. Start as you mean to go on.*

"As a matter of fact," she confessed, leaning in closer as if what she had to say was salacious gossip instead of simply embarrassing. And of course he would draw the worst conclusions—who wouldn't? "I am in some debt."

"Some?" His brow arched again, while his gaze seemed to pry into her. Any further, she thought in a mixture of that same dizziness and something far darker and more dangerous, and he'd be able to *see* the number itself like a tattoo inside her head.

"A great deal of debt," she amended. He only looked at her, and she smiled, though it felt strained. "A vast, impossible sum, as a matter of fact. Do they still have debtor's prison in England?"

"Not since the nineteenth century," Rafe said in that dry, not-quite-amused voice. "I think you're safe."

"From debtor's prison, perhaps," Angel said sadly. She was only partially faking the sadness. "But not from the appalling interest rates."

His gaze moved over her again, testing. Measuring. Once again, she felt like a show horse. She had the insane urge to show him her teeth, as must surely be expected in cases like these, but refrained at the last second.

"How do you imagine a marriage based on a transaction like this would work?" he asked then, as if, she thought in a potent mix of excitement and terror, he was actually considering it. Was he considering it? "For example, what do you have to bring to the table?"

"My spectacular beauty, of course," she said in very nearly the same matter-of-fact tone he'd used before. She might have been discussing show horses herself, she thought. Teeth to hooves. "I'd be an excellent trophy. And as we all know, rich men do love their trophies."

"Indeed." Again, that wicked brow. Arrogant. Powerful. He was not, she thought belatedly, a man to be trifled with. "But as we all also know, even the greatest beauty fades in time while wise investments only multiply and grow. What then?"

Angel had not anticipated actually having this conversation, she realized then. She certainly had not imagined being quizzed on *her* potential contribution to the marriage of convenience that was meant to save her. Possibly because she hadn't really expected that her brilliant plan, dreamed up in coach class over an insipid plastic cup of vodka orange, would go this far, she admitted to herself. Had she been kidding herself all along?

But no, she thought firmly. What, exactly, were her options? She might be enjoying this conversation with Rafe McFarland, Lord Pembroke, Earl of Great Wealth, far more than she'd imagined she might when she'd first seen him— but whatever the outcome, she was fifty thousand pounds in debt. And while her unreliable mother was the one who had got her into this, Chantelle was unlikely to be any help in getting her out. Sadly, she knew Chantelle entirely too well.

This was up to her to solve. On her own. Like everything else in her life.

"I am delightful company," she continued then, emboldened by her own panic.

She forced herself to smile as if she was perfectly at ease—as if she routinely rattled off her résumé to strange men as if she was up for auction. Which she supposed she was, actually. Not a cheering thought.

"I'm very open-minded and won't care at all if you have a sea of mistresses," she told him.

She meant it. She'd seen that in action with Bobby and her own mother, hadn't she? And it certainly seemed to work for them, as they'd been married for years now. Who was Angel to judge the way they conducted themselves and that marriage if they themselves professed to be happy?

"In fact," she continued, trying to pretend her mother's marriage didn't make her feel dirty by association, somehow, "I'd expect it. Rich man's prerogative and all that. I have very little family, so there will be no tedious holiday functions to suffer through and you won't have to lay eyes on them at all, should that be your preference."

She thought of the great, raucous Christmases with loving if careless Bobby and all the Jacksons with a sharp twinge of guilt. She thought of her stepbrother Ben's quiet concern and determination to be there for her whether she liked it or not, just as a brother would, she imagined, with another searing pang. Allegra's unobtrusive but steadfast support. Even Izzy. But she cast it all aside.

"I have a great many opinions and enjoy a good debate," she said, trying to think of the things an *earl* might want in a wife, and able only to picture those endless period dramas on the BBC, all petticoats and bodices and everyone falling all over their titles in and out of horse-drawn carriages, none of which seemed to apply to this situation. "But I'm also perfectly happy to keep my own counsel if that's what you'd like. I can be endlessly agreeable."

"You make yourself sound like some kind of marionette," Rafe observed. Not particularly kindly.

"If by that you mean the perfect companion and wife," Angel replied sweetly, "then I agree. I am."

She searched his face again, but saw nothing new. Nothing that told her if she was swaying him one way or another. Nothing that explained why she was suddenly so very determined that she should succeed in this. Only that strange, curiously *him* mixture of violent ruin and male beauty, so striking and imposing and impossible to look away from. Only that cool, measuring gleam in his dark gray eyes. She pulled in a breath, prepared to launch into another list of all she had to offer, whatever that might be, but he reached over and put a finger on her lips.

Bold. Hot. Shocking.

Something kicked deep inside of her, hot and low. She felt his touch like flame. Like a blazing light that seared through the darkness and made her shine too. Her head spun around and around, even after he dropped his hand back to his side.

"You can stop," he said mildly. Almost casually. "I'll marry you."

He didn't know what he expected her to do. Squeal with joy? Weep with gratitude? Naturally, Angel did neither.

She only watched him for a beat, then another, and he had the distinct impression that she was shocked. Stunned?

While he simply wanted her. Any way he could have her. If it would take a healthy application of his money, well, he had plenty of it, and he needed a wife besides. He told himself it was purely practical. And yet that *want* pulsed in him.

Still she gazed at him, as if trying to work something out.

Perhaps, he thought darkly, his money was not *quite* dirty enough to ensure her blindness to his scars after all. It hadn't yet prevented him from seeing the truth of himself either, and he knew more of that truth than she ever would. He could hardly blame her.

"Come," she said then, surrendering her empty champagne glass to a passing waiter and then holding out her hands. She did not smile, though her too-blue eyes began to gleam. "Dance with me."

Rafe did not dance. But then, he also did not propose marriage, however offhandedly, in crowded ballrooms to perfect strangers, much less those who had just shamelessly announced they were in the market for a rich husband— any rich husband, presumably. When he thought about it in those terms, he couldn't think of a single reason why he *shouldn't* sweep this odd, arresting woman into his arms as if they were lovers and perform the steps to a waltz he hadn't executed since the lessons his mother had insisted upon a lifetime ago.

But he would take any excuse he could get to touch her, wouldn't he? What, he wondered, did that make him?

She was graceful, warm and deliciously curvy in his arms. The small of her back curved enticingly beneath his palm, the fingers of her other hand were delicate in his, and she smelled of fresh flowers with a kick of spices he couldn't identify. She tilted back her head to look at him, and for a moment he only gazed at her. *So pretty,* he thought. And so surprising, when nothing had surprised him in far too long. It made her dangerous, he knew, dangerous *to him,* but he shoved the thought away with his customary ruthlessness.

"Out of curiosity," he asked, need and desire making him hard, making him fierce, "how many other men have you asked to marry you tonight?" He studied her face as he guided them across the floor. "I only ask in case there is some kind of battle for your affections I should prepare myself to fight."

"Not at all." Her expression was very nearly demure— and therefore wicked by implication. He felt the impact of it move through him, making him burn. Want. "You are my one and only." He was fascinated by her. And by his reaction to her. "But aside from my obvious charms, which, let's face it, no man could possibly resist, why do *you* want to do this?"

He let himself look at her for a long moment. The sharp blue eyes. The pretty face. The lush mouth so at odds with the quick, disarmingly honest words that came out of it. And her short, choppy blonde hair that, he realized, he wanted to drag his hands through as he angled that mouth of hers to fit his. He wanted that with an intensity that surprised him anew. He wanted it all.

He hadn't let himself want anything in years. But he wanted her.

And best of all, there was nothing hidden. No artifice. No murky agenda. No great pretense. She was in debt. She needed money and, he suspected, the security of knowing that there would always be more. Meanwhile, he needed a wife he did not have to woo. A wife who would not want things from him that he was unable to give—things that most wives would expect from a husband, but not this one, not if he bought her. She might see the monster in him, over the course of their time together, but she would be paid well to ignore it.

It was anything but romantic—and that was precisely why he liked it. And her.

He told himself it was just that simple.

"You are the first woman in years who has approached me as a man, instead of a desperate charity case before whom they might martyr themselves for an evening," he said quietly. He might know there was no man beneath his monstrous face, but she did not. And still she treated him like one. How could he resist it? "More often, they do not approach me at all. And I must marry after all. It might as well be a woman with no expectations."

She cleared her throat. "Oh, I have expectations," she said, and he wondered if it cost her to keep her voice so even, her gaze so light on his that he felt an echoing brightness inside of him. "But I feel certain you can meet them. You need do nothing more than sign the cheques to win my eternal devotion."

In Rafe's experience, few things were ever so easy.

"Since you have been so forthright, let me share my expectations with you," he replied then. He held her close, so close she could do nothing but stare directly at the scars that told the world who he was—the scars she would spend a lifetime staring at, should this odd, very nearly absurd conversation turn into some kind of reality. "You understand that I must have heirs."

"You great men always do," she said knowledgeably, her eyes bright with some kind of amusement. Then she laughed. "Or so I've heard. And seen in films."

He pulled the hand of hers he held to his chest, and understood, in that moment, how much he wanted this.

Wanted her. More than he could remember wanting anything—anyone—ever. *Because this is so convenient,* he told himself. *I need do nothing at all but accept.* He told himself he believed it.

But he knew the truth. It beat in him like a drum, thick like desire and as damaging, making him think he could have a woman like this, that what lived in him would not destroy her as it had destroyed everyone else he'd ever loved or wanted to love. That her need for his money would protect her, somehow, from his need for her.

She should be so lucky, he thought grimly, but he did not let her go.

"You are a beautiful woman, as we've agreed," he said in a low voice, his eyes hard on hers. "I imagine begetting the next generation will be no hardship at all for me—but you may have more difficulty with it." He let that sink in, and when he spoke again, his voice was gruff to his own ears. "I will try to be sensitive to your revulsion, but I am, sadly, only a man."

Was that a faint hint of color he saw, moving across the golden skin at her neck, her cheeks? Another quick shadow chased through the blue of her eyes.

"You are too kind." He felt himself stiffen as her gaze traced over the path of his scars again, sweeping across his face, impossible to ignore. He couldn't decipher what he saw in those marvelous eyes then, darker than before, and continued on.

"I don't like anything fake." He shrugged. "Thanks to my scars, I am unable to hide from the world. I dislike it, intensely, when others do."

"I've never been very good at hiding anything," she said after a moment. That smile spread over her mouth then, as tempting as it was challenging. It made him want to know her—to figure out what went on inside that head, behind that pretty face. *You play a dangerous game,* he warned himself. "What you see is what you get."

He doubted that too.

"Most importantly," he said, hearing his voice move even lower, and feeling her shiver slightly, as if in reaction, as if she felt him deep inside of her, or perhaps that was only his own fervent wish, "I am not open-minded. At all. I will care, very much, if you take a lover."

Again, that electricity, stretching between them, burning into him, making him forget where they were. *Who* they were. Who *he* was, most of all. She made him forget he was a monster, and he found he didn't know how to handle it. Or what it meant. And he squashed down, ruthlessly, the seed of hope that threatened to plant itself inside of him. Hope was pointless. Damaging. Better by far to deal in reality, however bleak, and weather what came. Better to banish *what if* altogether. It never brought anything but pain.

"No seas of lovers then," Angel replied, the faint huskiness in her voice the only indication that she was affected by this bloodless talk of sex. Perhaps she, too, was fighting off the same carnal images that flooded his brain. "And here I thought we would have a modern sort of marriage. I hear they're fashionable these days, all adultery and ennui."

There was a certain cynicism in her voice. He wondered what marriage she'd seen too closely and found so wanting. Not that it signified.

"They may be," he said darkly. He stopped dancing then, pulling them over to the side of the great ballroom, though it took him longer than it should have to let go of her. He wanted her that badly. It should have horrified him. "But I should warn you, there are two things I will never be, Angel. Modern or fashionable. At all."

He was warning her off, Angel realized, in a sudden flash of understanding. He had backed her into one of the grand pillars, and she felt it hard and smooth against her back with a sudden rush of sensation that was as much exhilaration as it was wariness. He was big and dark and entirely too dangerous, and she told herself it was reasonable nervousness that kicked to life in her veins, sending that wild shiver throughout her body. Nerves. Nothing more.

"Do we have a deal?" she asked softly. "Or will you keep growling at me until I run screaming into the crowd to find myself a more malleable rich man to proposition?"

His mouth softened, and she saw that flash of arrogance again, reminding her of how powerful he was. He was not, she could see, at all concerned that she might run anywhere. She would have found that somewhat offensive, had she had any intention of moving.

"Is that what I'm doing?" he asked, all aristocratic hauteur, eyebrow crooked high in amazement. "Growling?"

She reached over and laid her hand against the hard plane of his chest, carefully and deliberately. He was warm to the touch, and she had to fight back another shiver. Of nerves, she told herself again. This situation was extreme, even for her.

"We're talking about a marriage of convenience," she said. With some urgency, as if that might dispel the lingering darkness that she sensed hung between them. "Yours as well as mine. I don't expect you to sweep me off my feet while quoting *Wuthering Heights*."

His mouth crooked. It wasn't a smile, not really, but it made her feel absurdly glad, even so.

"You are so reasonable," he murmured. He reached up and took her hand, but kept it where it was, trapped tight against his chest. Was that his heart she felt thumping so hard, or was that her own pulse? "One is tempted to think you've had a run of convenient husbands."

"You will be the first," she assured him. "But who knows?

If it works out, it could be the start of a long and profitable line of husbands. I can collect them, one by one, and live on their tireless support until I'm a doddering pensioner."

"That is a lovely picture indeed," he said in that low voice, and it licked at her, making her think about *the begetting of heirs* and all manner of other things he made seem far more enticing than they should be simply by talking about them in that voice of his. And the way he looked at her, a dark fire in those deep gray eyes, made her chest feel too tight, her skin too small for her bones. "But let's concentrate on the one in front of you."

"Yes," she agreed, though something was happening to her. She couldn't look away. The hand that he held, flat against his wide, distracting chest, wanted...*wanted.* She felt light-headed. "Does that mean we're agreed? One perfectly convenient marriage, made to order right here in the middle of the Palazzo Santina?"

For a moment he only looked down at her, his scarred face harsh and his remote gray eyes cold, and she was suddenly much too aware that he was a stranger to her. A complete and total stranger, who she had asked to marry her in the middle of a crowded ballroom, in a country not her own, on what amounted to little more than a whim. How insane was she? How could this be anything but a disaster?

"Yes," he said. "We are agreed. We can marry as soon as you like."

Again, some sense of deep foreboding moved through her, shaking her. She would be far better off with some older, much less dangerous man, she thought in a sudden panic, someone she could manipulate with a smile and bend to her will. That would not be this man. That would not be Rafe. She knew it as well as she knew her own name. If she had any sense of self-preservation at all, she would call this off. Now.

But she didn't move. She didn't say a word. She had no idea why not.

"You look terrified." That single brow rose, pointedly.

"Not at all," she said, shoving the foreboding aside. Better to be practical, especially in her dire circumstances. She tilted her head back, invitingly, and gazed up at him. "But I feel the occasion calls for something, don't you? Something to mark such a momentous decision. How about a kiss?"

"A kiss." His voice was dark and disbelieving. Gruff. "This is no fairy tale, Angel."

She felt her own eyebrows rise then, in cool challenge.

"Then you have no need to fear you'll be turned into a frog," she replied tartly. His mouth twisted, but his eyes burned hot.

"As you wish," he murmured, mocking her—or perhaps both of them.

His hand moved from hers to hold her chin in an easy grip, as if her mouth was his already, before he'd even tasted it. And then he bent his head and captured her mouth with his.

It was a swift kiss, commanding and sure. Possessive and demanding, it seared into her like some kind of red-hot brand. She felt it storm through her limbs, lighting her up with that sweet and terrible electricity, making her lean closer to him, fascinated and captivated by the sure, carnal mastery of his kiss, the hint of more, of something dark and sweet and addictive—and then he pulled away.

Too soon. Much too soon—but then she remembered herself. Where they were. *Who* they were.

She felt herself flush with heat, and only just kept herself from squirming beneath that dark gray gaze. She felt out of control. Exposed. He let go of her chin and she staggered back against the pillar, unable to keep herself from raising a trembling hand to her lips like some kind of artless virgin.

Had that really just happened? Had he really just kissed her like that?

Was she really…shaking?

And looking at her, Rafe McFarland, Lord of All He Surveyed and soon to be her husband, finally smiled.

CHAPTER THREE

I⊤ WAS the memory of that smile, so unexpected and curiously infectious, lighting up that scarred face and making it something new, that Angel found herself playing over and over in her head as she headed back home to London and reality.

That and the kiss that never failed, even in retrospect, to make her uncomfortably warm.

It was simple surprise, she told herself—at the depth of her own response. It was nothing more than surprise that he'd had so much passion in him, and that she'd met it. And how could it be anything else, when the only thing between them was money? His money. Her need of it.

And your body, a dark voice whispered inside of her. *Isn't that always the way this kind of arrangement goes?*

"Here is my contact information," Rafe had said, all distance and business, in the car he'd summoned to take them back to their respective hotels after Allegra's engagement party had come to an end. He had jotted down a few quick lines on a card he'd pulled from somewhere. Angel had found herself admiring the bold, male handwriting, scrutinizing it as if it might give her some clue about the man. He'd handed the card to her when he was finished, his gaze once again dark and grim, no hint of that brief, flashing smile left anywhere on his ruthless face. As if she'd imagined it. She'd begun to wonder if she had.

He'd refused to take her details at all. Not even a mobile number.

"You may find that once you are back in London, and the royal Santina champagne has worn off, that you are less interested in going through with this after all." His gaze had been level. Matter-of-fact. Somehow, that had made it worse.

"I'm sorry to disappoint you," she'd said, stung. More offended, perhaps, than the situation warranted. After all, he was just being appropriately cautious—which perhaps she should have been herself. But in the dark, close confines of his car, she'd felt nothing but that current of reckless determination, driving her on, making this happen. *Because it had to.* Surely that was the only reason. Surely it was reason enough. "But I'm not drunk."

"We'll see," he'd said, and his expression had been very nearly bleak then, and had made something turn over inside of her. "I wouldn't hold it against you if, upon reflection, you decide that you must have been."

She'd flushed, with something she'd told herself was temper. Simple temper, nothing more. "I'm not drunk," she'd said again, distinctly. "But you can pretend I am, if that gives you the escape clause you clearly want."

"Ring me when you arrive in London," he'd said softly as the car glided to a stop outside her hotel. His gaze had challenged her. Dared her. And made her, somehow, unutterably sad. "Or don't."

Angel, naturally, had rung immediately, still fueled by that same temper. When the plane had landed in Heathrow and again when she'd reached her flat. To prove the point, she'd assured herself expansively, but to herself or to him?

"Oh, dear," she'd said into his voice mail the second

time, when she was safely home and just as determined, filled with something perilously close to righteous indignation. "It appears that two days later and without the champagne, I still want the marriage, just as I suspected I would. But I should tell you, Rafe—" and she admitted to herself, sitting there in her dark flat where no one could see her, least of all him, that she liked the way his name felt in her mouth "—that unlike you, I *will* hold it against you if you change your mind. Just to be clear."

And she did want this. Him. Of course she did. He was the answer to all of her prayers, she reminded herself fiercely and repeatedly. She would be rich and a countess to boot! All of her problems would be solved! Not bad for a wild fantasy on a plane ride and a single dance at an engagement party, she told herself. Not bad at all.

And if there'd been a gaping sort of hole inside of her, far too black and bitter for her to look at directly, she'd ignored it. Fiercely and repeatedly.

"I'm afraid I have urgent business I must attend to for the rest of the week," Rafe told her in that stern, aristocratic voice when he finally returned her calls, right when she was starting to believe that perhaps she'd fantasized the whole thing after all. Just made it up to take away the pain of Chantelle's latest and greatest betrayal, the way she had when she was a little girl—telling herself stories to make her nights alone less frightening while Chantelle was out with "friends". "I'm afraid I did not factor the possibility of a fiancée into my schedule."

That word. *Fiancée*. It made a chill sneak down her back and she wasn't sure why. What she was sure about was that she didn't want to know.

"Are you sure this isn't simply a test?" she asked, keeping her voice light.

She knew it was. She knew he was still making certain. Making absolutely sure that she'd meant every single word she'd said in that ballroom. Making her question herself and decide if this was what she wanted. If *he* was what she wanted.

Not to mention, deciding such things for himself. After all, he was bringing far more to this devil's bargain than she was. It was difficult to imagine, standing by herself in the middle of a flat in a neighborhood she doubted he'd ever visited or could locate on a map, why a man like him— *an earl,* of all things—would bother. There had to be any number of willing would-be countesses scattered about the country, no matter what he thought. Angel couldn't possibly be his only option, the way he was hers.

She hated how that made her feel. So…needy. Desperate. Two things she'd never felt before, not about a man. There was nothing about the feeling—itchy and unpleasant— that she liked.

She moved restlessly around her small, serviceable flat, her gaze skipping over all the detritus of this life she'd been so desperate to call her own, that she was now equally desperate to get rid of. All the books she'd hoarded, kept away from Chantelle's hoots of derision as she'd called Angel *Lady Muck*—each of them an escape, a fantasy, the education she'd denied herself. Surely wanting to leave the life she'd made, whatever might have become of it, spoke of deep deficiencies in her character. It had to. But then, what part of her behavior over the past few days did she think offered a counterargument?

"Not at all," he replied coolly, snapping her back into the conversation. "But it is, of course, a period for reflection and research. I suggest you avail yourself of it."

"Reflection and research?" she echoed, and then laughed. *Keep this light,* she reminded herself. *Easy.* She ran her fingers over the spine of one of her favorite books, an old classic involving titled gentlemen, intricate revenge plots and all manner of epic adventures. "I think you'll find I'm an open book. Written in very simple and easy-to-read sentences."

"But I am not," he replied, with what might have been dark humor, had he been another man. There was a pause, and she wondered where he was. What he was doing. What sort of room he stood in, having this bizarre conversation with a woman he hardly knew. Did he regret this already? Did she? Why couldn't she tell her own feelings where this man—this situation—was concerned? "You may live to wish you'd taken this more seriously, Angel."

"Yes, yes," she said dismissively, her voice far more blasé than she actually felt. "Marry in haste, repent at leisure. Etcetera. I promise to think hard and deep about the ways in which your money could alter my life for the better, for as long as you think it necessary."

"You do that," he told her in his serious way, his voice all cool command and dark authority over the phone. And, she thought, somewhat disapproving too. She didn't like how much that bothered her. "I will send for you on Monday morning. We'll discuss the ramifications of this arrangement then, in detail and with my solicitors."

"And what if I want to speak to you before then?" she asked, more to see what he would say than from any current burning desire to have access to him. And in any case, it was only Tuesday morning now. Monday was a long way away. It was going to be difficult, she thought, to have a savior in hand yet still out of reach. To be still smack in the middle of her life, with her problems, while the new and far better, far easier life dangled just beyond her fingertips.

She might very well go mad.

"You seem remarkably adept at leaving extraordinarily

long voice-mail messages," he replied silkily, and she felt it like the sharp reprimand it was. "I imagine you will have no trouble whatsoever leaving more if you feel it necessary."

She stood there near the front window of her flat, the phone in her hand, for a long time after he ended the call. She stared out toward the street, her heart beating hard and too fast, seeing nothing at all but the future she'd conjured up out of sheer bloody-mindedness, pure shamelessness… and her big mouth.

Maybe she'd taken this whole make-your-own-fairy-tale thing a bit too far.

She imagined that was a common enough reaction when you suddenly found yourself in an actual palace, stepsister to a real, live Cinderella. And when faced with Allegra's happily ever after, complete with an island kingdom and a handsome Prince Charming, it was perhaps understandable that Angel had conjured up fantasies of modern-day princes who would dance off into bliss and happiness with a common girl like her, all choirs of tweeting budgies and swelling, rapturous soundtracks. But that was the shiny, happy Disney version, wasn't it?

There was also the rather more dark and dangerous Grimm Brothers version, which she'd spent perhaps too much time reading as a lonely, largely ignored child. In that version of *Cinderella,* as she recalled, birds did not so much sing pleasing melodies as peck out the eyes of the nasty stepsisters. The famous glass slipper was filled with blood. The woods in the original fairy tales were always perilous, filled with wolves and menace, and she had no idea what on earth she was playing at with a man like Rafe.

"Oh, Angel," she said out loud, her voice shaky in the quiet room, and as rough to her own ears as if it was a stranger's. "What the hell are you doing?"

* * *

It was much too late at night, and yet Rafe was awake, staring at the sheaf of photographs spread out across the wide expanse of the platform bed he sprawled across. The pictures chronicled Angel's entire sporadic modeling career, in glossy color and intense black and white—one pouty-mouthed, mysterious-eyed, loose-limbed shot after the next, helpfully supplied by his legal team for his review.

"Your future countess," Alistair, the lead solicitor, had intoned in his habitually contemptuous way when he'd handed Rafe the folder. With a derisive flourish.

He shouldn't have liked the way that sounded. He shouldn't have felt that fierce need move through him again, wanting her in all the ways he could not let himself want anything.

She was so distractingly beautiful. But, of course, that was irrelevant here. He of all people should know how little outside beauty had to do with anything. He'd been aware of that stark truth from a very young age. The scars on his face now were incidental at best. They paled in comparison to the ravaged remains of the rest of him, and well did he know it. He had the ghosts to prove it. His entire army unit. His whole family. He never forgot a single one of them. He felt them all like deep, black holes where his heart should have been. He wore them like regret and recrimination where others wore only bone and skin.

He knew exactly what kind of monster he was.

He rose from his bed and moved restlessly to the tall windows that looked out over London, a city he loathed deeply but hardly saw tonight. He saw only her face. That insouciant smile. The sharp intelligence in her gaze. The heat of her touch. Her delectable mouth.

He knew better than to want her—to want anything—this much.

A good man would not have let this happen, no matter

how tempting she was. A decent man would have ended it the moment they were back in London, back to reality. He might not have been either one of those things, but he knew there was still a part of him that longed to be what he should have been, what he'd never been. There was still a part of him that dreamed, sometimes, that he could be better.

If he was any kind of man at all, if there was any shred of humanity in him, he would not let her chain herself to a ruined creature like him. She didn't know any better—but he did. She saw only bank balances and some kind of savior, but he knew that was only the tiniest part of what she'd get—of what she'd have to endure. He carried the weight of every single person who had ever been close to him. Surely Angel deserved better than that. Better than him.

But he couldn't seem to make himself do what he knew he should.

He told himself that she knew what she was getting into, or near enough. She was marrying a perfect stranger, for money. He told himself that only a woman with extremely low expectations could possibly consider such a course of action. He told himself that theirs would be a practical business arrangement, with possible side benefits, perhaps, but one that would never, could never, involve *feelings* of any kind.

It was important to make all of that clear from the start. He wanted a marriage that was shot through with the cold light of reality. He wanted duty and obligation, responsibilities and rules. That would keep the monster in him at bay. That would curtail the inevitable damage.

He was doing this because it was more honest, he told himself. He was not promising her anything. She was not pretending to be in love with him. They would both get exactly what they wanted out of this, and nothing more. Surely that would keep her safe, if nothing else.

He put his hand against the windowpane then, letting the cold glass seep into his skin, reminding him. Who he was. What he could do. What, in fact, he'd done. The cold turned to a numbing kind of pain, of punishment and penance, and still he held his palm there, determined.

This was not about hope. It was about need.

All he had to do was remember that.

It was Friday when Angel saw an unexpected picture of herself in one of the horrible tabloids, tucked up next to Rafe as they'd headed toward his car after the engagement party on Santina. It crystallized her thus far shaky resolve to finish this thing before it really started. To call it off, as she'd been closer to doing every day. That was, she'd decided, the only sane thing to do.

She stood staring at the grainy photograph for far too long in the aisle of her local off-license, as if she expected it to divulge the secrets of her own heart right then and there. As if it could.

The girl in the picture had her head tilted invitingly as she gazed up at the dark, dangerous face of the man next to her. Even in a cheap and sleazy tabloid, Rafe was impressive—too much so—and Angel looked, she was embarrassed even to think, entirely too much like her money-grubbing, social-climbing mother, a connection the tabloid was quick to make itself. It made her cringe in shame, and then redden with deep embarrassment. And it brought home the unpleasant reality of what she'd set out to do.

What she was, in fact, doing.

The entire world would know that she was marrying Rafe for his money, just as Chantelle had married Bobby for his money before her. And they would be right. They would call her all those terrible names, like *opportunist*

and the far nastier *gold digger. And they would be right.*
She might as well simply give in now and accept that she
was her mother, after all these years desperate to be anything but.

And the truth was, she didn't think she could live with
that. With herself, if that was who she became, no matter
her reasons. She pushed her way out of the shop, making
her way back down the street toward her flat, blinking
back the emotion that rushed through her so unevenly and
threatened to spill out from behind her eyes. She was a
mess—she could feel it in every cell of her body—but she
still refused to let herself cry. She *refused.* How many ways
could she betray herself before there was none of her left?

A phone call from Ben, her would-be big brother, only
made it worse. Her steps slowed as she answered, and she
forced herself to adopt her usual flippant tone. It was harder
to do than it should have been, and she didn't want to think
about why that was.

"What are you doing with the Earl of Pembroke?" Ben
asked directly, in that way of his that reminded Angel that
he did, in fact, worry about her. And about all of the many
Jacksons, as if worrying was his foremost occupation, in
place of his usual world-conquering.

It made her stomach clench in shame, around another
bitter surge of panic. What would she tell him? How could
she face him again if she did this crazy thing? Ben had
never wanted anything but the best for Angel, however unlikely that seemed, given the cards she'd been dealt and the
choices she'd made. This would disappoint him, deeply, as
he was one of the few people who Angel had ever let get
somewhat close to her. Because he had, despite her best
efforts, she opened her mouth to tell him what was really
happening.

But she couldn't bring herself to do it, to tell him the

truth. She realized she couldn't quite bear to say it out loud. Not to Ben. Not to someone who would care, and would be so very *sad* for her. That made it all so squalid. So desperate and pathetic, somehow.

She mouthed something careless and shallow instead, hardly aware of what she was saying. What did it matter? When she got home, she would call Rafe and end this madness, and none of this would signify.

"Be careful, Angel," Ben said. It made her throat feel tight. As if he could see. As if he knew. But he didn't, she reminded herself. He couldn't. He'd only seen that terrible photograph, which didn't even show Rafe's scars, and certainly didn't show Angel's true, mercenary colors. It was, in all the ways that mattered, a lie.

"I always am," she replied lightly, and while that certainly wasn't true, what was true was that she survived. She always, always survived. So what else really mattered, in the long run? It was better than the alternative. "He's rich and titled, Ben," she said then, interrupting him as he tried, yet again, to step up and fix things in a life that, she was afraid, could never be fixed, not really. And certainly not by Ben, dear though he was to her. It meant more to her than she could say that he still tried. "What more could I want?"

That question rang in her head after they'd talked for a few more moments, after she'd evaded his questions and waved away his concern, and after she'd slipped her mobile back into her pocket for the remainder of her walk home. The April day was cold and gray, with a blustery sort of wind that made Angel feel empty inside. Spring seemed like a fairy tale itself on the chilly London street, an unlikely story at best. She tucked her chin into her warm wool scarf, and had her head bent against the relentless slap of the cold, and that was why she didn't see the slender, tousled-blonde-headed figure standing at the door to her building with a cigarette in one hand and a newspaper in the other until she was very nearly on top of her. When she did, her breath left her in a great *whoosh,* as surely as if she'd been kicked in the stomach. Hard.

Chantelle.

Of course.

"Aren't you the dark horse," Chantelle said in her insinuating, insulting way, lounging in one of the chairs in Angel's tiny kitchen as if she was perfectly comfortable there, which, Angel reflected balefully, she undoubtedly was. Having no shame at all removed all manner of discomforts that others might feel in similar circumstances, she imagined. Chantelle had not bothered to put out her cigarette outside, and so still smoked it, even as she tapped the tabloid that she'd flung on the table between them with the restless, manicured fingers of her other hand. "An earl, no less! You've learned a little something from your mother after all."

"Do you have a cheque for me, Chantelle?" Angel asked pointedly, unwinding her scarf and tossing it with far more force than necessary toward the empty chair. "Because I know this can't be a social call. Not when you owe me fifty thousand quid with interest mounting by the day."

Chantelle blew a stream of smoke into the air. "No wonder I didn't lay eyes on you once in Santina," she said, as if Angel hadn't spoken. As if what she'd done wasn't hanging between them like an ugly screen. "I thought you were avoiding me, but the whole time you were holed up with his lordship playing—"

"How could you?" Angel said tightly, cutting her off. *"Fifty thousand pounds?* What could you possibly have been thinking?"

She told herself that her mother looked abashed then,

but she knew that was wishful thinking at best. Chantelle didn't know the meaning of the word. Angel had learned the truth about her mother over the years, whether she'd wanted to or not. Over and over again.

"It was an accident," Chantelle said now. Just as she always did, her voice slightly husky as if she was in the grip of strong emotions. Which, Angel reminded herself angrily, she was not. She had no emotions—only the ability to feign them. "You know I'll pay you back, love. It was just a little bit of help to tide me over."

"You won't pay me back," Angel said flatly. As much to herself as to her mother. "You never do."

"It won't matter, will it?" Chantelle replied without missing a beat. "You could be a countess soon enough, if you play this right, and what will you care about money then? You'll have pots of it."

She made no effort to disguise the tinge of bitterness in her tone, much less the avaricious gleam in her eyes— bright blue eyes that were identical to Angel's. Angel hated the fact that she so greatly resembled this woman. It horrified her that anyone believed she was anything at all like her—and she knew they did. The whole wide world did.

Even she did, if she was honest. And hadn't she walked up to Rafe at that party and proved it? Like mother, like daughter. It made her throat burn with something like acid.

"You can't possibly imagine that after stealing my identity and sticking me with a huge bill, I'd be likely to give you any money should I marry into it, can you?" Angel made her voice incredulous when, really, she wasn't at all surprised. Chantelle twitched herself up from the chair opposite and moved toward the sink to toss her cigarette butt away. Leaving a soggy mess for Angel to clean up, no doubt. Like everything else she ever touched.

"I raised you all on my own, Angel," Chantelle said

without turning back around. Her voice was wistful. Something like nostalgic. And was, Angel knew, no matter how much she wished otherwise, entirely fake. "I was only eighteen when I had you, and it wasn't easy."

She wished, for only a moment, that her mother was someone, anyone, else. Someone who might say the things Chantelle did and mean them. Even once.

"Does it count as 'on your own' when there was a parade of men in and out of the door at all times?" Angel asked musingly. "Some were simply your lovers, I suppose, but others were honest to goodness sugar daddies. Which I suspect is just another way of saying *married,* isn't it? Just like my father?"

"Some daughters in your position would be a little bit more grateful," Chantelle continued, only the hardening of her voice any indication that she'd heard Angel at all. "I made the best choices I could for you, when I was barely more than a child myself."

"Chantelle, please." Angel laughed, entirely without humor. "You were never a child."

"Because I had no choice," she retorted. "I had to make do, didn't I? How else would you have been fed?"

Chantelle twisted around then, and Angel met her mother's gaze. So blue, so bright, and so endlessly conniving.

"Why are you here?" she asked quietly. "I know you're not going to pay me back. I even know you're not going to apologize. So what can you possibly want?"

"Can't a mother drop in to see her own daughter?" Chantelle asked, her blue gaze guileless. Which meant she could be up to anything at all. Anything and everything. "Especially when you haven't answered your mobile in days?"

"I know how this goes," Angel said, too weary even for bitterness. Too numb, she thought, and was grateful for it.

It made everything easier. What hurt the most was when she actually believed that Chantelle could change—that she even wanted to try. How many times would she fall for that? After all these years? "You'll keep at it until you say something that makes me feel guilty. Then you'll work that until I end up making you feel better for what you've done. Until I've apologized for what *you* did to *me*." She shook her head. "You do it every time. It's like clockwork."

"Such airs you put on," Chantelle said, her gaze as hard as her voice. "You might as well be a flipping countess already. Don't forget, I know the truth about you, Angel." She nodded toward the newspaper on the table. "We're no different, you and me. I'm just a little bit more honest about it."

"You don't know the meaning of the word *honest,*" Angel snapped. "You've never even brushed up against honesty in passing."

Chantelle sniffed. "I can see you're determined to make this hard," she said loftily, as if she was rising above Angel's childish behavior through sheer goodness, great martyr that she was. "I want you to remember this, Angel. You take such pleasure in making me the villain, but I'm the one who came round this time to sort things out, aren't I? And you won't even give me the time of day."

"I gave you fifty thousand quid, *Mum,*" Angel retorted. "Without even knowing it. Without you even asking. I'm all out of things to give you, and I mean that literally. I have nothing left."

She wasn't surprised when Chantelle slammed out of the flat, but she was surprised that she didn't find herself nearly as destroyed by one of her mother's always upsetting and depressing little visits as she usually was. She pulled the newspaper toward her again, and stared down at that lie of a photo.

What wasn't a lie was that Rafe was so solid, so surprisingly tough, and it was visible even in newsprint. That soldier's way of holding himself, strong and unbendable, perhaps. She had the feeling that he was the kind of man—notably unlike her stepfather, Bobby, and most of the population of London, including some of her own early boyfriends back when she'd been foolish enough to bring them into Chantelle's lascivious orbit—who would see a woman like Chantelle coming from miles off and be singularly unimpressed. It made her feel warm again, imagining his complete imperviousness to a woman like Chantelle.

It would be like Chantelle didn't even exist.

He wasn't promising her happiness. He was promising her financial security. And it dawned on Angel as she sat there, the smell of Chantelle's cigarette smoke still heavy in the air, that the only kind of happiness she was likely to get in this life would involve protecting herself from Chantelle and her games. And the only thing that could guarantee her that kind of protection was money. Pots of it, as her mother had said. If she was really, truly rich, it wouldn't matter what Chantelle did. She could protect herself, and pay it off without blinking if somehow that protection failed. Chantelle would never again be in a position to ruin her life—she wouldn't even have access to it.

The very idea made her feel freer than she had in years.

Maybe it was better to be alone as she'd always been, but nevertheless financially safe with someone who accepted her on the level they would arrange together, than plain old alone *and* prey to her mother's endless schemes. That was why she hadn't let herself ask Ben—himself no slouch in the money department—for help, because he would have helped her, but Chantelle would only have done it again. And again. And how many times did she think her stepbrother could step in? He could only have been a temporary fix. Marrying Rafe was a long-term solution. He was signing up in advance to pay her bills. And, unlike Ben, at least he was getting something in return.

She wanted to be free of Chantelle, no matter how terrible a daughter that made her. For once in her life, she wanted Chantelle to have no reach, no influence. For once. *For good.*

She thought of Rafe's ruined face, and the wild flare of passion that had made her shake. That demanding kiss, the one that still haunted her. That had kept her awake and panicked throughout the long week. That threatened her in ways she was afraid to contemplate too closely. She already knew it would not be easy with him. It might even be bad—there was every reason to think so. They were strangers. They had nothing in common as far as she could see. The potential for disaster was huge. Almost guaranteed, in fact.

But it would be different than this, and she would have some protection, at long last—and who cared what she had to barter to get it? She wasn't unaware of the irony inherent in this choice she was making. It seemed to lick into her like some kind of terrible poison, making it hard to breathe: in order to escape her mother, she would have to become her. She would have to do the very thing she'd always sworn she'd never, ever do.

She knew she should come up with some other solution—any other solution—but the truth was, she was out of solutions. She felt flattened by this latest stunt of Chantelle's, and some part of her was terrified to find out what lay on the other side of this feeling. If anything.

The truth was, Angel was so very tired of just surviving.

Of always having some new tragedy to get over.

She was tired of living by her wits, of making do.

She was tired of digging herself out of messes she hadn't even made.

She was tired.

And what did it matter what people thought of her? They already thought it. They had for years. Let them.

It had to be better with Rafe. She told herself it just had to be.

Because the truth was, she thought as she moved over to the sink to find her mother's ashes and swollen cigarette end lying there in a wet, smelly mess across the bottom of the basin, like everything else Chantelle had ever touched, anything was better than this.

CHAPTER FOUR

Once Rafe's mandated week of reflection and research was over, and Angel's decision made, everything seemed to pick up speed. Angel imagined that she would meet with Rafe himself to go over the details of their marriage that Monday morning, as arranged. She also imagined that there would be a few papers to sign and even fewer actual details to discuss. After all, they'd agreed to the marriage of convenience itself. The marriage made of money and future heirs, no romantic notions need apply. Surely *that* was the hard part?

She was wrong on all counts.

"No second thoughts then?" he asked her, his dark voice low and stirring even over the phone. Angel held her mobile too close to her ear and pretended that she felt as serene as the lushly appointed leather expanse of the backseat of this luxurious car should have made her feel, but, strangely, did not. "If you do not come to your senses now, Angel, you will soon be trapped with little hope of escape."

"You should really consider going into some kind of marketing should the earl thing not work out for you," she replied, summoning that light tone out of the ether. She even chuckled slightly. Warmly. "You do paint such a lovely picture."

"I want you to remember that I warned you off," he said, his voice a low growl.

But all she could think of was his cold gray gaze, and the shocking heat of his mouth against hers, the ache of it winding through her even now, in a different country and without him anywhere near her. What was the matter with her?

"I feel sufficiently warned," she assured him. "If you turn out to be the Earl of Bluebeard, killer of wives who should have known better than to appease their curiosity, then I have only myself to blame."

"Just so long as we're clear on that point," he said silkily, and disconnected the call.

Angel held the phone in her hand, the sleek mobile hot to the touch, and pretended her heart hammered against her ribs as it did because of the ghastly London traffic on the streets all around her. Because of the traffic, and not this mix of fear and expectation, anticipation and—she could scarcely admit it to herself, she could barely allow that it was true on any level—desire.

She thrust that from her mind. For the rest of the drive she braced herself for the impact of seeing him again—and was not at all prepared for the rush of disappointment she felt when she didn't.

He wasn't there to meet her. He wasn't there at all.

That first day, and every day that week, she met with a team of solicitors. At least eight of them, gathered around the large, gleaming, probably ancient and frighteningly expensive table in the elegant dining room of Rafe's extremely fashionable town house in a neighborhood of central London so impossibly wealthy that hereditary fortunes seemed to hang in the air, like ripe fruit on bountiful trees.

Angel had felt distinctly underdressed and unworthy simply exiting the sleek silver car when it rolled to a stop at the curb. As if the pavement itself rejected the likes of her. As if the neighborhood was judging her as she stood there, trying not to gape about her in awe and a kind of anticipatory wonder; as if the desperately lofty Georgian town houses that ringed the famous and well-photographed square, with their impressive facades and storied, monied histories, were looking down their figurative noses at her and her grand plans to rise so far above her station.

She knew that was all in her own head. She was equally certain, however, that the forbidding and encompassing censure of the assembled collection of solicitors was not.

"I thought I was meeting Rafe," she said when she took the seat she was waved into with something just short of actual courtesy, and looked around at the blank wall of uniformly condemning male faces. She was only happy that her voice remained steady.

"We are the earl's legal team," the most visibly disapproving, most outwardly judgmental one said from his position at the head of the scrum. "We are here to represent the earl's interests and, naturally, to protect yours." His fine, patrician nose let out a single, pointed sniff, a veritable masterpiece of judgment swiftly and irrevocably rendered. "Miss Tilson."

Angel smiled thinly, feeling far more raw and exposed than she should. More raw and exposed than she'd ever allow herself to show these haughty, self-important men.

"No need to say my name as if it hurts your mouth," she said sweetly, leaning against the stiff back of the chair to brace herself, knowing full well it would look casual and assuming to the men frowning at her. "It will be *Countess* soon enough."

Upon reflection, it did occur to her that a comment like that no doubt cemented the entire legal team's already low opinion of her in one fell swoop. But there was no taking it back, and she told herself it was better to get on with the whole of the inevitable judgments and the snide glances from the start. The excruciatingly chilly reception of the solicitor brigade was, after all, a pale shadow of the reaction she could expect from the press. From the world. *Like mother, like daughter,* and so on.

So she simply accepted it. And signed.

And signed.

There were reams upon reams of documents. Towering stacks of them. Many, many duplicate copies. There were contracts to go over clause by mind-numbing clause, and then question and answer periods for each one of them. Yes, she understood the meaning of the word *dependant.* No, she did not foresee any issues arising from compliance with rider B, clause 8. And on. And on. There were a thousand little details before the Eighth Earl of Pembroke could marry that, apparently, had to be raised and then handled accordingly by a fleet of trained professionals assigned to each separate, extremely overanalyzed minor point in question. The definition of adultery. The consequences thereof. The schooling of any and all heirs. The discharge of debts.

Her debts, to be clear.

Cheques were written to Chantelle's credit card company, and to the letting agency that rented Angel her flat. Angel was required only to sign where bidden to sign, and to divulge all the information requested when asked for it. Her entire financial as well as personal history, for example, while the phalanx all around her took copious judgmental notes and requested additional documentation.

It was all so practical, so cold-blooded, Angel thought, on something like the eighth day, sipping at the tea that was perpetually at her elbow, always steaming hot, and always accompanied by a tempting array of small, perfectly formed pastries. The constant perfection of the tea and pastries reminded her why she was doing this, should the wall of dreary dark suits all about her tempt her to forget. The tea and pastries represented the perfect, carefree life she was about to start living, for which this purgatory of papers was no more than a necessary precursor.

And this approach to a marriage put everything on the table, didn't it? Why suffer through the traditional trials of the first year of a marriage when it could all be dealt with so efficiently in advance? You only had to check your more tender feelings at the door, and every possible area of future contention between you and your spouse-of-convenience could be ironed out well before any vows were exchanged.

What could be better? she asked herself. What could be more rational, more reasonable? She was delighted with herself that she was approaching this new phase of her life in so pragmatic and thoughtful a fashion. *She was.*

"I was under the impression that British courts did not, historically, look kindly on prenuptial agreements," she said at one point, as she eyed yet another stack of papers in front of her.

"There is significant debate on that issue in the legal community," the nearest lawyer snapped.

Angel only smiled.

She told herself she didn't mind when she was trotted off to Rafe's personal physician and asked to subject herself to a comprehensive set of physical exams, including a great battery of blood tests and other more sensitive procedures. She didn't ask what they were testing for, because, of course, she knew. How had it never occurred to her to wonder about how this side of things would work? She shouldn't be at all surprised. Naturally, Rafe wanted to be sure that she was both fertile and disease-free. He wanted to get his money's worth, didn't he?

She had absolutely no reason at all to feel hollow inside, she told herself fiercely. Every night when she was home alone in the flat that looked dingier by the day, and every morning as she sat in the back of a car so expensive its price had made her gag slightly when she'd looked up similar models online. She had signed up for this. This was what this kind of arrangement looked like. It was all very thorough. It made sense.

This was, at the end of the day, exactly what she wanted. Wasn't it?

She saw him, finally, almost ten full days into the tests and contracts and explanation of clauses. Angel walked through the high-ceilinged foyer of the distractingly elegant town house, leaving for the day after having spent hours signing away her rights to any and all fortunes that Rafe might or might not settle upon the children they might or might not produce in the course of their marriage, which might or might not last any significant amount of time. Over and over again, on all the necessary copies. Just as she'd done every day so far, in one form or another.

He did not speak. He only stood in the arched doorway to what she'd been told was a reception room of some kind. She might not have seen him at all, so completely still was he, and so fully did he blend into the darkness of the unlit room behind him. But she felt an odd shiver skate down the back of her neck. She turned her head, and just like before in the ballroom of the Palazzo Santina, there was nothing at all but his cool gray gaze.

She stopped walking. She slowly pivoted. Without meaning to move, she took a step closer to him, then caught herself. He stood there in the doorway, watching her, more solid than she remembered, as if he stood firm and commanding on the ground. As if he demanded no less than that from the air he breathed. *Ruthless,* she thought, and had no idea where that word had come from. When had she ever seen him be anything but kind, if, perhaps, severe? No matter how he hinted he might be otherwise?

It was that pervasive sense that she was in danger, the frantic pulse in her veins, the low curl of adrenaline that set up a kind of humming beneath her skin, that made him seem so much larger than life. So much darker, so much bigger, as if he could dwarf the world with his cold gray eyes alone.

"I had started to wonder if you were a figment of my imagination," she said, speaking before she knew she meant to, automatically adopting that airy tone, as if the very sternness of his ruined face demanded it. "It never really occurred to me that there were so many practical matters to attend to. You always imagine it's just straight from the romantic dance to the happily ever after, don't you? No ten days of contracts to sign, just a cheerful song as the credits roll."

He didn't appear to move so much as a muscle. And still it was as if he moved closer, towered over her. She swallowed, hard.

"Have you convinced yourself this is a romance, Angel?" he asked in that dark way of his, that seemed to settle into her bones and shift like some kind of flu through the rest of her. Hot. Cold. And back again. "I fear you have set yourself up for a grave disappointment."

She smiled. She had the strangest feeling that if she didn't, if she showed even the faintest hint of the confusion or panic inside of her, he would call this all off. And she didn't want that. It was amazing how much—how strongly and how deeply—she didn't want that. Far more in this moment, she realized in some surprise, than before.

"If I had," she said, so casually, as if she felt nothing at all but a lazy sort of passing interest in this conversation, "the past ten days would certainly have cured me of it, wouldn't they? I assume that was the point."

Another long, dark pause. His brows lowered. That grim mouth was set in an implacable line. Angel could not seem to stop reliving the feel of it against her own. She thought, suddenly, with a flash of searing heat, of their wedding night. Would they have one, in the traditional sense? Did she want to? Would she feel this man against her so soon? *In her?* Why did the prospect make her feel short of breath?

"It may not seem so to you," he said gruffly, "but I am seeking to protect you as much as me."

"I am the woman who marched up to you at a ball and asked if you'd be so kind as to let me marry you for your money," Angel replied, letting her smile deepen, shoving the lurid images of a possible wedding night aside. She let her smile grow infectious. Very nearly merry. She didn't understand the part of her that longed—there was no other word for it, to her confusion—for him to return it. "I don't think I really need protection from you. From myself and my insane little scheme? Very possibly—yet here you are going along with it against, I am sure, all legal advice." She raised her brows. "Maybe I should ask your battalion of attorneys if *you* need protection from *me*. I suspect they think you do."

Rafe had thought of very little but this woman.

He was a busy man. He came to London as seldom as possible—he hated this dirty, sprawling city as much as his disreputable brother had loved it, with all of its ceaseless noise and all of those pitying, prying eyes—which meant he had to cram as much business as he could into the short span of time he was actually in town.

But business was nearly impossible to conduct when all he could think about was Angel. That clever gleam in her too-blue eyes and the answering, knowing sort of curve to her wicked mouth. That perfectly curvy body that today made a pair of denim jeans into a blessing, clinging to her hips and outlining her beautifully shaped legs. It took him long moments to drag his attention to the drapey sort of black sweater she wore, the sort that usually seemed to require endless fiddling and arranging. Not that Angel was doing either. She merely watched him.

He worried that she saw far too much. Or not nearly enough. He couldn't decide which was worse. She was marrying him for his money, and he was marrying her because she'd done such a good job of pretending he was not the monster he knew full well he was. And because he could not seem to help but want her—so much so it consumed him. It ate at him.

It made him wish that things were different—that *he* was different. It made him *hope*.

He'd expected her to back out of this, as any sane person would. And every day she did not—he hoped a little more. And that hope was more dangerous to him, more treacherous and insidious, than anything else could be. He knew it.

But he could not seem to stop it.

"I am more than adequately protected," he said shortly. Far more shortly than was necessary. "As the number of attorneys present in your sessions should indicate, I have no intention of losing my family's wealth and consequence. For any reason."

"And certainly not to a gold-digging tart like me," she said in that dry yet amused way, though her blue eyes were suddenly unreadable. "I hope you found the results of my physical examination to your liking."

He knew there was a reprimand there. He could sense it, despite her light tone of voice and her easy, open expression.

"Do you expect an apology?" he asked softly.

"Not at all," she said at once, though he didn't quite believe her. But she smiled in that way of hers, that made him want to respond in kind, that made him *feel* things he was determined he could not feel. That he certainly shouldn't allow himself to feel. "I was presented with your relevant medical records this morning. Allow me to congratulate you on your good health, Lord Pembroke. Long may it last."

"If you want an apology," he said evenly, feeling more solicitous of her than he should, than was wise, when he knew he had nothing inside of him, nothing to give, "you need only ask for it. I may or may not tender one upon demand, but you should know that I certainly don't appreciate the passive-aggressive approach. Ever."

He imagined he could hear her heart beat then, loud and fast in the hushed quiet of the hall, or possibly he only wanted to believe he affected her in such a way. That she reacted to him at all. He took far more satisfaction than any kind of good man would have in the faint color that stained her cheeks.

"I think this is our first argument as an engaged couple," she breathed, and he had the sense that she was far angrier than she was letting on. That she was hiding all manner of things beneath that tough exterior of hers. It should have concerned him—but instead, he found he only wanted to see what was underneath. "A milestone."

He wanted to see what was behind her breezy manner, her seemingly effortless confidence. He wanted to see her. He wanted to *see* her in a way he'd never wanted anything, not in more years than he could recall. He hardly knew what to make of it. Maybe that was how he found himself moving from the doorway and into the hall, until he was standing much too close to her.

And it was still not enough.

"I told you how little interest I have in masks," he heard himself say.

"We all wear masks, Rafe," she replied. Was that temper in her breathless voice? Or was she warning him that she already saw through his mask of scars to the far uglier parts of him that lay beneath? "Some of us have better reasons for that than others, but the most you can expect is that people try to be honest with you despite whatever things they might need to hide behind. Or you might find you have to explain your own mask."

He didn't want to talk about masks, especially not his own. Her blue eyes seemed to darken the closer he stood to her, and once again he had the near-uncontrollable urge to bury his hands in her short, choppy blonde hair and drag that mouth of hers to his. He wanted to take and take. He wanted to glut himself on her.

Hell, he just wanted her. However he could get her.

He had been furious at himself for that since that night at the Palazzo Santina. He was no less furious now. He wondered what, exactly, showed on his face, because she swallowed then, and he had the sense she forced that cocky little smile of hers.

"I'm speaking figuratively, of course," she said softly. Lying. He was sure of it, and he couldn't seem to care as he should. He wanted her to participate in this dance, this delusion. He wanted her to be a part of it too. "The *figurative* you. Not the *actual* you."

"What a great comfort," he said, his own voice dry.

He wanted to reach over and pull her into his arms. He wanted to strip away her clothes and test the perfection of her curves with his palms. *He wanted.* He was all too aware that she was prepared to fulfill certain obligations in this cold-blooded marriage of theirs—and that none of those obligations had anything at all to do with this *need* that rolled through him, distracting him and infuriating him. He contented himself with the smallest touch, just the finger of one hand, tracing the bloom of color against her cheekbone. He felt her slight shiver, quickly checked, like a dark triumph deep inside of him.

"And is that what I can expect then, Angel?" he asked quietly, his voice a low rasp. "Your honesty?"

"Of course," she said, her voice little more than a whisper, her eyes wide and locked to his.

He wanted that to mean more than it did, more than it could. He wanted that faint shiver he felt to be all of the things it could never, would never, be. She treated him not like a monster, but as a man, and he found that was more dangerous, more potentially ruinous than all the other women who had recoiled in horror at the sight of him. They'd been fooled by the ugly surface into thinking that was what made him monstrous. But Angel ran the risk of learning the truth.

He should never have let this get so far. He should end it now.

But instead, he traced a pattern along her cheek, and pretended he was whole.

"I'm sure I signed something to that effect," she said.

Those perfect brows arched high. Again, that easy, insouciant smile that captivated him far too easily. That made him believe in all manner of things he knew better than to trust. That made the little flare of hope light anew, small but sturdy. And brighter all the time, heaven help him.

She smirked. "In triplicate."

Angel Tilson married Rafe McFarland, the Eighth Earl of Pembroke, a man she wondered if she knew less now than she had when she'd met him, if that was even possible, on a gray spring day that was wet and dark and the precise color of his cold eyes.

It was precisely three and a half weeks since the day she'd met him at Allegra's engagement party in the Santina royal palace. She wore a dress of deep, midnight blue, like the summer night sky far in the north, far away from this quick, quiet ceremony in a London registry office. It was the least bridal, least *gold-digging* sort of garment she'd been able to come up with from her closet, having declined numerous offers from Rafe's staff to find her *something appropriate to the occasion.* Angel had been determined to go to her wedding, at least, in a dress that was entirely hers. As nothing else would be when this day was over.

Rafe was dressed in another glorious, obviously hand-tailored suit, all somber colors to match the fierce expression he wore on his scarred face. The suit clung to the hard planes of his body and shouted to all and sundry that he was exactly who he was: the head of a great family, steeped in generations of wealth and privilege. More than that, there was a soldier's hard steel beneath it all, that seemed stamped into his very bones. The way he stood, still and sure. The way his gaze met hers, demanding and challenging.

Angel didn't look away. She hardly heard the words the registrar spoke; she barely registered the presence of the two members of Rafe's legal team who stood by as their witnesses. But she was *aware* of him, of Rafe, as she'd never been aware of anyone else in her life. She saw every one of his scars, saw the flat line of his hard mouth, and understood with a deep certainty that this was an irrevocable act. That no matter what happened from this day forward, she would never be free of this hard, watchful man, not really.

She supposed that should have terrified her, but it didn't.

That, in turn, did.

As if he could sense it, his mouth curved slightly in the corner as he spoke the necessary words.

"I do solemnly declare that I know not of any lawful impediment why I…" and he intoned his full name then, with all his unnecessary middle names, the ones his solicitors had insisted she learn in their precise and proper order. His eyes never left hers. Daring her, Angel thought. *Daring* her to give in to her fears and end this right now.

Would she? For an impossible, breathless moment the panic surged through her and she almost turned and ran for the door.

But she didn't. She only pulled in a breath as Rafe continued.

"May not be joined in matrimony to Angel Louise," he said, finishing his part of the declaration. His dark eyes said something else entirely, something Angel was afraid to translate.

Angel repeated the words back to him, aware now of the heat in her, the flush across her cheeks and even lower, making her breasts feel heavy. Making her whole body feel hectic. Something like frantic. Her legs seemed to tremble beneath her even though she knew they were holding her steady, because she did not fall.

None of this should matter, these things she felt and the difficulty she seemed to have in pulling in a deep breath, but it did. It all mattered, suddenly. The deliberately blank expressions of the witnesses. The impartial and disinterested tone of the registrar's voice. The bare room, really more of an office, empty of any bridesmaids, flowers, music, family. Anything that might make this wedding a joyous event instead of a dry business arrangement.

This was the very last thing I wanted, a voice cried out in the quiet of her mind, all of those vows she'd made to herself when she was younger cascading through her then, taunting her with how far she'd fallen and what she'd become, but it was too late for that. It was much too late. Fifty thousand pounds and twenty-eight years of Chantelle's brand of mothering too late.

And then she was saying the rest of those words, those old, traditional words that so many brides had said before her, in cathedrals and in churches, in stately homes and in registry offices just like this one, so many of them filled with love and hope and a whole spectrum of emotions she did not expect she would ever feel. Some part of her grieved, even as another part was strangely exultant. She felt torn—ripped between parts of herself she didn't even understand.

They joined hands. Angel felt the jolt of it, the pull. She worried that he could feel the way she shook, but when she looked at their hands clasped together like that, like a real couple's, she couldn't see the evidence of that shaking— she could only feel it on the inside, making her very bones seem to rattle in place.

Rafe spoke then. He said *thee* and then he said *wife* in that low, gruff voice, and then he slid a ring, the metal cold and heavy against her skin, onto her finger. She couldn't even look at it. She could only look at him.

You will soon be trapped with little hope of escape, he'd told her in that same voice, and she could see, now, the doors of that trap shutting all around her. What it would mean, this loveless marriage. What she would give up.

She would be safe, she told herself, like some kind of chant. She would be free. There were better things, she thought, than love or hope or emotions that had no place in decidedly and deliberately practical arrangements like this one. More useful things, by far.

And still, she did not look away from him. Still, she

gazed back at him, accepting his dare—throwing out one of her own. She knew she was doing it—she saw the awareness of it in his dark gaze—and she could neither stop herself nor seem to figure out what, exactly, she thought she was doing.

Marrying him, she thought, with something very like humor, dark and twisted though it seemed to her in that moment. *I am actually marrying him.*

"I call upon these persons here present to witness that I, Angel Louise, take thee," she said then, as she was meant to do. And again, as she paused to breathe and then speak his name once more, there was nothing but Rafe and that cold, frozen sort of patience in his gaze. He made no move to coerce her, to convince her. His hands held hers easily, with that same stillness that made some kind of bell chime in her, deep and low. He only watched her, his ruined face carefully stiff as if he was ready for any outcome at all. She believed it. "To be my wedded husband," she said, finishing that ancient phrase, and she was astonished to hear that she was whispering. That her voice was shaking as if she was timid. As if she was someone else.

It was that word, she thought in a dazed sort of amazement. *Husband.* She hadn't been ready for *that word.*

She slid the ring they'd given her earlier onto his finger, felt him clench the hard muscles of his hand slightly as she did so, and then it was done.

It was done.

She jerked slightly when the registrar said "husband and wife", as if she'd already forgotten that it was them, that it was *her,* that this was who they were now to each other. *Husband and wife.* She felt something very nearly like dizziness, as if she'd had too much champagne, when the truth was, she could hardly remember the last time she'd had a drink. Certainly not today. That might make it look as if there was something to celebrate.

"You may kiss the bride," the registrar said then, jolting Angel back into the moment. Back into *her wedding*.

She smiled at Rafe, and it was harder than it should have been to make her mouth curve in that easy way that she knew she needed it to do. Much harder than she expected, but she did it. She had the insane notion that the only thing standing between her and some kind of desperate oblivion was that smile, however crazy that might sound even in her own head.

Rafe did not smile back. His gaze was hard, unflinching. Angel expected another brief, searing sort of kiss like the one in the palace. She felt that shivery heat move through her, heating her up from the inside out in anticipation, making a wicked flame bloom and pulse in all of her secret places.

She wanted that kiss. God help her, but she did.

He took one hand and slid it against her cheek, capturing her that easily. For a moment there was only that searching, somehow implacable look in his eyes, and then his mouth lowered to hers.

And there was nothing at all but fire.

That grim and perfect mouth was demanding against hers, forcing her to open to him, to submit to him, to throw herself heedlessly into this dance of flame and need between them.

By the time it occurred to her that she should not allow this—that she should try to save herself from this thing between them that she couldn't seem to control or deny, that would, she knew on some level she could not understand, destroy her in some fundamental way—he was pulling back.

His hard palm still curved against her cheek, more

brand than balm. And she loved it. The shock of *that* seared through her like that same, edgy need for him that still echoed in her, much as she told herself that it had to be something—anything—else.

But there was no denying that gleam in his gray eyes, that hint of silver that she recognized immediately. It was pure male satisfaction, and it hummed through her, making her breasts ache and her core melt. She let out a shaken sound she pretended was no more than a breath and his serious mouth curved.

They turned to sign the register, and Angel took it as an opportunity to pull herself together. She didn't know why she was so fascinated by this man. *Her husband.* She didn't know why he had such a powerful effect on her. But she did know, beyond any shadow of a doubt, that the papers she had signed did not allow for this. It was one thing to marry a man for his money. That was a cold, practical decision. It was another to *want* him like this. What would that make her, if she succumbed to it? What kind of fool married for mercenary reasons and then *felt things* for her husband? Worse, what would he say if she told him that she thought she'd made a mistake—that she wished she'd approached him another way? What would he do if she said she wished they'd got to know each other, done this properly? She nearly cringed, imagining the look on his serious face.

How would he look at her if she admitted that she wished that this was romantic after all?

She was such an idiot. She felt the truth of that snake through her, making her stomach clench. And then she looked at him, this husband who would never see anything when he looked at her save what she cost him.

His guard had dropped into place again, that quiet curve of his mouth no more than a memory—she could see it as plainly as if he'd pulled a helmet of hammered armor over his face. Once again, he stood stiff and ready, that cold bleakness in his gaze. It was the same way he'd looked at her as she'd approached him in the Palazzo Santina.

Waiting, she realized in dawning understanding, and something else that made her chest feel dangerously hollowed out from the inside. He was waiting. For the harsh rejection he must have learned to expect. For her to prove to him once again that he was the monster he believed himself to be—that he'd told her he was.

You will soon be trapped with little hope of escape, he'd said, because he thought that he was the thing that went bump in the night. That he was what she feared, instead of the trappings of this bargain they'd made, and what she knew it made her that she'd suggested it in the first place. And then taken it. And then, worse by far, gone and started to feel things she never should have let herself feel.

And Angel could not bear it. She could not add to this man's pain. They were only scars, she thought, and yet he'd clearly been treated terribly because of them. And whatever else he was, or would be to her—and her mind skittered away from examining that too closely—she simply couldn't be part of the great weight he carried around and wore like a badge of fierce pride, as if he expected nothing less.

She simply could not bear it, no matter the cost to herself.

So she smiled, and it was easy this time. Easy and bright, and she reached over and took his hand again, as if she had every right—which, she supposed, she did now. And would, for as long as this devil's pact between them lasted. She ignored the darkness in his gaze. She ignored the rush of panic that threatened to tip her over where she stood, because none of this was what she'd wanted once, and she

knew that what she did now would seal this marriage—
would trap her just as he'd warned—more surely than any
kiss ever could.

Even a kiss like his.

Beneath the panic there was something else, something
hot and dark and his, and while she had no idea what would
become of her, that part didn't care. It only wanted more.

She smiled down at their signatures, then at him. And
she laughed.

"Well, look at that," she said, and she found she was
carried away in her own merriment, suddenly. As if she'd
made it real. As if it was true, this sudden light feeling
that could, in other circumstances, have been some distant cousin to joy. Or perhaps not so distant after all. "I'm
a bloody countess."

CHAPTER FIVE

"Your belongings have been packed up and moved out of your flat," Rafe said in his gruff way, breaking the silence that had grown thick between them. "As planned."

The wide and plush back of the sleek silver sedan seemed significantly less roomy with Rafe in it. He sprawled on his side of the seat, his long legs eating up the space before them, the heft of his big body—that wide, hard chest and those strong arms—seeming to encroach upon her when Angel knew, rationally, that he wasn't moving. He didn't have to move to take up all the space, all the air. He simply did. As if he exuded too much power to be contained in his own body.

He watched her, those dark eyes moving over her face like a touch. Like the touch she could still feel, that set her heart racing and made her breath shorten in her throat.

The truth she didn't want to face seemed to expand inside of her, making her feel as if she might explode.

"Wonderful," she replied, forcing the appropriate smile, hoping it looked duly appreciative.

She made herself relax against the seat, then made herself look at him too—as if nothing irrevocable had happened, as if nothing was sealed or set in stone or any of the other overly dramatic and frightening things she'd told herself during the actual ceremony. Anyone might get carried away during a wedding. She wasn't a machine, after all. Of course she had feelings—she'd married this man! She could wish that things were different between them—that they were different people, who had gone about this in a very different way—without acting upon that wish. Who knew what she would actually feel, once the wedding day itself was over? Once they made it through whatever their wedding night might hold? The intensity of the occasion had simply got into her head, she reasoned. That and the seriousness of it all, of what she'd agreed to as she'd said those words. Understandable, really, that the enormity of this—of the huge, extraordinary step she'd taken with this man—would take a bit of processing. With or without her inconvenient desire for him.

Her smile felt less forced, suddenly. "I've never moved anywhere without having to spend day and night packing up boxes and making endless arrangements," she said then, her voice deliberately light to dispel the tension in the very air between them, thick and treacherous. "It never occurred to me that it could simply *happen* while I was off doing other things. Wealth really does make everything so very *convenient,* doesn't it?"

That ghost of something not quite a smile played with his hard mouth, and seemed to call out shadows in the cold gray of his gaze.

"It has its uses," he agreed in that low voice that vibrated along the length of her spine. That single brow of his rose, dark and aristocratic. Demanding. "It has brought me you, has it not?"

"My goodness, Lord Pembroke," she said softly, keeping that easy flirtatious tone in her voice. She found that she did not have to force herself to relax against the seat then—that she did it without thought. "Has the ceremony gone to your head? Do you think this is a romance?"

She took entirely too much pleasure in throwing his own words right back to him. Especially given what she'd been feeling all morning.

His dark eyes lit with something appreciative and purely male, and the way they met hers, so bold and knowing, made Angel's heart stutter in her chest. She was sure he moved closer then, she was sure of it, and she leaned toward him as if drawn by some dark compulsion she couldn't even see—but then he turned away, dropping the dizzying force of his attention to the mobile buzzing in his pocket.

Angel told herself she was relieved. She was. She wanted no part of this…mad whirl of sensation she couldn't even name, much less begin to understand. It all felt too big, too impossible. It was too dangerous by far.

Liar, that little voice whispered. What was dangerous was her reaction to him. What was impossible was this overwhelming urge to simply sink into him and disappear. But this wasn't a romance. There would be no happily ever after, not in the classic sense. If they were lucky, they would manage this union well, and get along with each other. Maybe even become friendly. That was all she should hope for.

That was all she could allow herself to hope for.

Rafe spoke into his phone, his voice clipped and sure, and she tuned him out, looking out at the passing London streets. Everything was going to be fine. Of course it would.

Today, it was all real—that desperate scheme she'd cooked up in her wildly uncomfortable coach class seat, on her way to see her favorite stepsister become a real, live princess. Her wildest imaginings had come true. She was married to an earl. She was a countess. She remembered Rafe's dire warnings as they'd danced in the Palazzo Santina, Allegra's engagement ball and the usual Jackson family antics no more than a blur to her. That he was not modern. Or fashionable. Or, if she recalled correctly, open-minded.

But what did that matter, really? He was an important man. A busy one, if his current conversation was any indication. She could soon be busy too, putting the generous monthly allowance he'd placed into an account with her name on it to excellent use around London. No more waiting around, cobbling together what paying gigs she could find, hoping she made the rent this month. Those days were over. That life was finished.

She could make herself over completely into one of those Sloane Rangers she'd never quite had the money to wholly emulate, flinging herself in and out of Harvey Nicks with a charge card in her hand and nothing more important on her mind than her next lunch date. She could even become one of those fixtures on the London charity circuit, forever attending this or that ball, draped in fabulous gowns and envy-inducing jewels, mouthing platitudes to every reporter she encountered about the great philanthropic work she was doing in all her couture. She was newly rich, and had married a pedigree. She could choose any life she wanted, surely. She could *buy* it, come to that.

And only contend with her husband—she still wasn't used to that word, and wondered if she'd ever be, if it would ever simply be a *term* she used instead of something more like a bomb—on the odd occasions they crossed paths. Which, if she knew anything about busy men with great amounts of wealth, a subject she had studied in some detail for some time, as it happened, would be increasingly rare as time wore on. That was how these marriages worked, no matter what claims Rafe might have made about how *unmodern* he planned to be.

She folded her hands together in her lap, and only then remembered that she now wore a ring on her formerly bare finger. Once she noticed it, it was impossible to ignore the alien feeling of metal and stone on her hand, digging into her flesh. For the first time, she looked down at her hand and really took a close look at the ring he'd put there.

It was stunning. As was, she reflected, every single thing of his she'd seen, from his suits to his car to his lovely town house. Of course the ring was gorgeous. The man, clearly, had exquisite taste. He was far too good for the likes of her, Angel knew, and the truth of that seemed to twist inside of her in a new, unpleasant way. She concentrated on the ring instead.

A large dark blue, square-cut sapphire rose above a bed of gleaming diamonds and platinum. One ring of diamonds circled the blue stone, while two other rings of diamonds sat on either side, though lower, each circling another, bigger diamond. The dark blue center stone glittered softly as Angel turned her hand this way and that, and something about it seemed to echo deep inside of her, hitting hard at that same well of sensation Rafe seemed to arouse in her so easily.

"It suits you," Rafe said, breaking into another surge of panic—surely it was panic this time, and none of that far more dangerous desire—that was rushing through Angel, making it hard to breathe. She was almost grateful.

"It's beautiful," she whispered, unable to look at him. Too afraid of what he might see if she did.

"It was my grandmother's." There was something in his voice then, some kind of emotion. She didn't know how to respond to it. She didn't know why she wanted to, with an intense and sudden surge of that same protectiveness as before. "I'm glad it will finally be worn again."

"Do you have your mother's ring as well?" Angel asked.

She didn't realize that was, possibly, an impertinent question—impolite, at the very least, when she'd only meant to make a bit of conversation—until his silence made her glance over at him. His face was shadowed. Dark.

"Sorry—" she began, but he shook his head.

"My mother gave her wedding rings to my older brother," he said after a moment, his voice entirely too calm. And distant. "They had a similar aesthetic, while my sensibilities were always more closely aligned with my grandmother's—my father's side of the family."

Angel had the sense he was choosing his words carefully. Then she focused on the most important word.

"Had?" she echoed hesitantly. She was conscious, suddenly, of that same urge she'd felt in the registry office. She did not want to cause this man pain. Even with an innocent question.

"They both died some time ago," Rafe said matter-of-factly, any emotion she might have sensed gone as if it had never been, hidden away beneath his scars. He shifted slightly in his seat, turning to better face her, the stern set to his mouth discouraging any further comment. "Is it really the time to discuss our pasts, Angel? We are already married. Perhaps it would be better to let them lie."

There was a kind of menace in the air then, simmering in the close confines of the backseat. Or was it simply a kind of warning? Either way, Angel ignored it.

"I insist that you tell me about your former lovers," she said expansively. She felt that she had to dispel the strange tension that seemed to hover between them, as dark as the day outside the car, or sink into it without a trace. "All of them. I want to know everything, so if we run into any of them at any point in time, I will have access to all their salacious details while I am pretending to be polite."

"I am fascinated that you assume my former lovers are the sort of people we will be running into at all," Rafe said in a dry voice. "I don't know whether to be complimented or insulted."

"And yet you show no interest in mine?" Angel shook her head. "That is certainly no compliment."

That brow arched high. "My interest in your former lovers is directly related to your medical records," he said. "Had they been anything less than pristine, we would have had a very different discussion."

In a different marriage, Angel thought, eyeing him, she might have been tempted to loathe him for that remark. But he was only being practical. Depressingly, insultingly practical.

"I am most definitely insulted," she said. "And not about medical records." She waved a hand in the air. "It's about the appropriate level of flattering jealousy, Rafe. I do require a *little bit* of it. It's only polite."

He gazed at her until her smile faded slightly. Then his hand moved, slow yet sure, and he reached up to brush a thumb across the curve of her jaw, the swell of her lips, sending a slow, sweet burn spiraling through her.

"You work so hard to be provocative," he murmured, his eyes so dark, his ruined face so intent. "What if I were to take the bait, Angel?"

She pulled in a ragged breath, finding it harder to gather herself than it should have been, and still his hand traced patterns against her skin, dousing her in his particular brand of fire.

"I would wonder why you were so easily provoked," she replied, her voice as uneven as her breath. His dark gaze was consuming, connecting hard and hot to something deep inside of her, making her feel as if she was melting. She could *feel* him—as if they were already naked, as if he was already inside of her, that powerful body moving over hers, driving her right over the edge—

"I will assume, as any gentleman would, that you are entirely untouched," he said. He dropped his hand back to his hard thigh. His dark brow rose again, mocking her. "To be polite, of course."

"Gentlemen and their virgins," Angel said, as if the topic were one she had discussed endlessly and been bored by years ago. "What vivid fantasy lives you men have."

"It is less the fantasy life and more the fragile ego," Rafe replied, amusement gleaming in his dark gaze. "I think you will find the history of the world far easier to comprehend when viewed through the filter of male insecurity."

"That is certainly true of my personal history," Angel said dryly.

"You are a virgin bride," he reminded her in that silky tone of his. "You have no personal history. Do try to keep up."

Her lips twitched, and Angel looked away from him, fighting the urge to laugh in a decidedly indecorous, un-countess-like manner. She looked out of the windows again instead, a certain warmth moving through her that had nothing to do with desire. In its way, it was far more dangerous. It promised too many things Angel knew she'd be better off banishing from the lexicon of possibility in this marriage. It was better not to hope, she told herself again, more fiercely this time. It was better to keep her expectations as low as possible. She knew that.

It took a moment or two of watching the world slip by on the other side of the rain-splattered window for Angel to make sense of what she was seeing. She blinked. The congested city streets had given way to the smooth expanse of the M4, headed in very much the opposite direction from the Pembroke town house in its graceful, historic square in central London.

"Why are we on the motorway?" she asked, bewildered.

Rafe only looked at her when she turned back to him, his expression unreadable, his mouth again in that impossible line. A trickle of something too much like foreboding, and far icier, began to work its way down the nape of her neck. She fought off a shiver.

"The London town house is not my primary residence," he said, with no particular inflection. His voice was still like silk, wrapping its spell around her, tempting her to simply sink into it. But she couldn't process what she was hearing. She couldn't take in what it must mean. "I spend the majority of my time at Pembroke Manor. We're flying to Scotland today."

"Pembroke Manor," Angel repeated dully as her mind raced.

Dimly, she remembered fiddling with her tea and trying to remain alert while one of the solicitors had droned on about "the Scottish estate." But had he said where it was located? Scotland was a rather large and varied place, which she knew primarily from the telly and that one ill-advised trip with her debaucherous friends to Aberdeen in her wild youth, best left forgotten.

There was all that…empty land, she thought with a shudder, just stretched out there at the top of the map of the United Kingdom, all icy lochs, impenetrable accents and ancient ruins scattered about the desolate landscape. On the other hand, there was also the beautiful, graceful city of Edinburgh, or the bustle and life in vibrant Glasgow. Neither city could compete with all of London's attractions, of course, but Angel was sure she could learn to make do. Somehow.

Even so, "Scotland?" she queried, just to make certain that was what he'd said. As if perhaps there'd been some mistake.

"The Scottish Highlands," Rafe corrected her, dashing

her hopes of anything resembling a decent nightlife. Or shops worthy of her new rank and net worth. Or entertainment of any sort at all, aside from all those caterwauling bagpipes and the odd kilt. "Lovely place."

"Remote," Angel choked out, visions of barren mountainsides, isolated lochs, endless fields of heather and precious little else dancing in her head. "Extremely and famously remote."

He only watched her, entirely still save for that wicked left brow, which rose inexorably as he gazed at her. It occurred to her, as it should have from the start, that he had done this deliberately. He had waited until it was already happening before he'd even told her it was a possibility. She couldn't think about that—about what it meant. For her and for her future. For her life. Not now. Not while her head was still spinning.

"Rafe," she gasped out, the panic taking hold now and making her stomach clench as surely as it made her flush in distress. "I can't live in the Scottish Highlands! It might as well be the surface of the moon!"

The part of her that wasn't swept away in the horror of the *very idea* of a city creature like herself condemned to some forced commune with the natural world that had never held the slightest appeal to her noticed that Rafe seemed to grow even more still, even more quiet.

"It is the ancestral seat," he said softly. *Dangerously,* that distant part of her noted, but it was thrust aside. "It is home."

"You must be mad!" she breathed. She waved a hand, indicating herself. She even let out a short laugh, trying to picture herself, all ruddy cheeks and jolly hockey sticks, milking a cow or shearing a sheep or whatever it was you did while slowly dying of boredom on an earl's rural estate. She couldn't manage it. She couldn't even come close.

"I am not at all suited to rustication. *Clearly.* I've never lived outside the city in all my life, and I have no intention of starting now—especially not when you have that lovely town house sitting idly by!"

"Unfortunately," Rafe said in a tone that indicated it was unfortunate only for Angel, "this is not negotiable."

He might as well have slapped her. Hard.

Angel felt herself go white, as reality asserted itself yet again. And it was harsh.

"Part of what you signed was an agreement to live where I live until any heirs we produce are of school age," Rafe said in that cool way of his, as if he did not care one way or the other, but was simply reciting the facts. "I promised you I won't rush you into the physical part of our arrangement, and I'll keep that promise." She felt his voice like another slap, so cold and sure when she was coming apart, when she was fighting so hard to keep from falling to bits all over the floor of the car. "I have no problem maintaining separate addresses in future if that is what you want, but not until the question of heirs is settled. And I apologize if this distresses you, but until then we will live at Pembroke Manor, with only occasional forays into Glasgow and even fewer trips down to London."

Too many thoughts whirled through Angel's head then, making her feel slightly sick. There was a heat behind her eyes that she was desperately afraid might be tears, and she knew that if she unclenched her hands they would shake uncontrollably.

And none of that even touched the storm that raged inside of her. It didn't come close.

How could she have forgotten the truth about this relationship? How could she have tried to protect this man, tried to shield him from hurt, when she should have known he would not do the same? Because why should he? This was a cold and calculated arrangement, not a love match. Not even a *like* match—as they'd hardly known each other long enough to tell! Why had she let herself lose sight of that for even a moment?

Why was there a part of her—even now—that wanted it to be different when it so very clearly wasn't and would never, could never, be?

He did not want her by his side at all times because he was swept away in emotion, which might have been forgivable, no matter how confining. No, he demanded it for the oldest reason in the world—because he wanted to make sure that any heirs that might turn up were his, and he had no particular reason to take her word on that subject or any other subject, because they were total strangers to each other. And she had no right to complain about that, or even about the fact he was whisking them off to Scotland in the first place, because this was the deal. This was what she'd signed up for—literally. She got access to his money. He got to make the decisions.

She hadn't imagined how difficult it was going to be to swallow those decisions when he handed them down. *You fool,* she chastised herself with no small amount of bitterness. *You pathetic fool—what did you expect?*

"And what if I can't do it?" she asked, not surprised to hear that her voice sounded like a stranger's. So far away. So thin. *Desperate,* she thought. She didn't look at him, but then she didn't have to. He still occupied twice the space that he should have done, all that power seeming now to pollute the air around them.

"You can leave any time you like," Rafe replied evenly. Angel noted that he did not sound unduly concerned about that possibility, though she thought she heard a faint undertone of challenge, even so. "But I feel compelled to remind you that should you choose to do so, you leave only with what you brought into the marriage. Your debt will remain intact, but instead of owing a credit card company fifty thousand pounds and any accrued interest, you will owe it to me."

He made that sound distinctly unappealing.

"I think I'd prefer to take my chances with the institutionalized usury actually, when you put it that way," Angel managed to say, with some remnant of her usual tone.

"As you wish," he replied, as he had once before, his tone very nearly mild. She hated him for it. "You need only speak up and we can end this arrangement right now."

She wanted to. Oh, how she wanted to! But that would be cutting off her nose to spite her face, so Angel said nothing. Rafe, meanwhile, shrugged with utter unconcern, as only a wealthy man who would never have to make such decisions could, and then he pulled out his mobile again and began to scroll through his messages. Dismissing her that easily.

Leaving Angel to fight a sudden war with herself, to keep those tears from spilling over her cheeks. To keep from flinging herself out of the car to appease the syrupy panic that kept growing ever tighter inside of her. To keep herself right there in her seat, beginning—too late, of course, she was always too late—to understand exactly what it was she'd done.

It was long after midnight, and Rafe stood out on the small rise some distance above the manor house that nestled between the thick woods on one side and the loch on the other, separating the Pembroke estate from the mountains that dominated the land by day. He could only sense them now in the stillness of the night, great masses hovering high above the land, as only the faintest wind moved through the sky above him and shivered its way through the trees.

He loved this land. He loved it with a desperation and a

certainty that knew no equal, that allowed for no comparison. He felt that love like a fact, an organic truth as relevant to his existence as the air he pulled into his lungs, the hard-packed earth beneath his feet. He remembered well his early childhood in these woods, Pembroke land as far as the eye could see, backing up to national parkland along the northern border. He'd spent long hours with his beloved father as they walked this land together in those happy years before his father's death, silently exulting in each pristine step they took into fresh snow in winter, or pausing to note the full burst of bright yellow gorse in spring.

Those days had been the happiest of his life. They'd been *before*. Before he learned the truth about the rest of his family, and how little they had cared for him. Before he'd lost everything that had mattered to him in the army. Before he'd accepted the dark truth about himself.

His gaze moved from the inky black woods around him and the night sky crowded with stars above to the manor house below him. For a moment he looked at the still-lit window of the countess's chamber, once occupied by his own mother, as it had been by every Countess of Pembroke before her, and the wives of the lesser lords the family had boasted before they'd been elevated to the title. He wondered what she was doing, his reluctant wife, in that room he'd avoided for years now, ever since his mother had died. He wondered if Angel would ever forgive him for dragging her, so urbane and sophisticated, to a place she must consider the worst backwater imaginable. A thousand miles from nowhere.

He wondered why he cared. He had not married her to please her. Quite the opposite, in fact—he'd married her to please himself. He was not at all comfortable with the notion that one might be dependant upon the other.

He shoved the uncomfortable thoughts aside and focused instead on the east wing of the manor. Or what was left of it.

"How amusing of you to fail to mention that when you spoke of your *manor house*," Angel had said in that dry way of hers upon their arrival, stepping from the car to frown up at the house before her, appearing impervious to the Scottish chill with the force of her impertinence, "what you really meant was *part of* a manor house. You may wish to disclose that little tidbit to one of your future wives before you present them with the great ruin they are meant to call home." Her smile had been touched with the faintest hint of acid. "Just a thought."

"I'm glad to see you've regained your spirit," he'd replied in much the same tone. "And that sharp tongue along with it."

"I certainly hope the roof holds," Angel had continued in that razor-sharp tone, magnificent in the cold light, her blue eyes piercing and the prettiest he'd ever seen. "I neglected to pack my carpentry kit."

It was not a ruin to him, he thought now as his mouth curved slightly at the memory of her words, and would not be until the last stone crumbled into dust. Nonetheless, he could not argue the point. Scaffolding had just been raised, but it couldn't mask the fact that an entire wing of the manor house was a burned-out husk of what it had once been. All of those centuries, gone in an evening. Priceless art and objects, to say nothing of some of Rafe's best memories—of lying in his father's study on the thick rug near the fireplace, reading as his father worked at the wide desk that had dominated the far wall. All of it so much ash, scattered into the woods, the wind.

He would build it again, he vowed, not for the first time. He would make it right—he would make it what it should have been.

He supposed there was something wrong with him, that he could not mourn what surely ought to be considered the greater loss in that fire—his brother, Oliver. Perhaps he was more the monster than he'd imagined, but he looked at the blackened remains of the manor and felt…nothing. His brother had been drunk, as ever, and careless, as usual. The investigators assured Rafe that he had felt no pain, that he had been entirely insensate as the wing burned down around him, taking him with it and making Rafe lord of what remained. Rafe supposed that was some small mercy, but he could not seem to grieve over his brother's wasted life as he thought he should.

Perhaps, he reflected as he looked at what was simply the most glaring example of his brother's carelessness, it was because he'd been mourning the waste of Oliver's life for as long as he could remember. He'd watched it all—the gradual decline, the increasingly erratic behavior. It had been like a particularly unpleasant echo of their mother's own alcoholic spiral, which had ended in a similarly unnecessary fashion in an alcohol-induced stroke which had been, by that point, a kind of mercy. It was difficult to mourn at the end of that road when he'd fought so hard to prevent it ever having been taken at all, to no avail. When he had only ever been ignored—or jeered at—for his pains.

He thrust the unpleasant family memories aside, and pushed his hands deep into the pockets of his heavy coat. He started walking again, this time back toward the manor house and his own bed. His footsteps were loud in the quiet of the night all around him. His breath made clouds before his face, then disappeared.

Again, his gaze moved to that window, still lit against the dark.

Today, Angel had married him and then looked at him like he was the monster he knew himself to be as he dashed her hopes of a London life in that car. He found that, some-how, the former eased the blow of the latter, and imagined that very thought made him that much more of a bastard.

"I will go insane in the country," she had said to him when they were aboard his private plane, winging their way toward the north. She had been sitting there so primly, her entire body rigid, as if she was holding back a tidal wave of reaction by sheer force of will. He had been impressed despite himself.

"You said you've spent your whole life in the city," he'd replied, not sparing more than a glance from his newspaper. "The charms of the country may surprise you."

"I don't mean that in a conversational, descriptive sort of way," she continued in that same very deliberate tone. "I don't mean I will feel restless or bored, or cranky. I mean that all of that emptiness—broken up only by the occasional flock of sheep—will drive me over the edge. I mean I will literally descend into madness."

He'd supposed he would have no one to blame but him-self if that were true. But then, he had ample practice in that regard, didn't he?

"The manor house has extensive attics," he'd said in-stead, looking at her over the edge of his paper. "Ample room for all manner of psychotic breaks and raving mad-women, I should think. No need to worry."

She'd been quiet for a very long time. When she'd spo-ken again, her voice was smooth. He'd wondered what that had cost her.

"How delightful," she'd said, her voice arid. "You've truly thought of everything."

Heaven help him, he thought now, staring up at her win-dow like some moon-faced adolescent in one of those un-bearable melodramas, but he wanted her.

He supposed he would pay for that too.

CHAPTER SIX

HE FOUND her in the library, of all places, his brand-new wife who had perhaps taken his talk of madwomen and attics far too much to heart. She'd become like a ghost in his house in the two weeks they'd been here—and Pembroke Manor already had more than its fair share. So did he.

She did not hear him enter. The library was a vast cavern, made bearable in the depths of the long northern winters only by its dual fireplaces, one at each end, and the bookshelves that lined the walls and seemed to wrest warmth from the cold stone. Rafe had spent innumerable hours here in his youth, lost in stories of lands far, far away from this place—and far away from what remained of his family after his father's death when he'd been only ten.

Angel sat near the far fire in the old leather armchair that had always been Rafe's favorite, her legs curled up beneath her, all her attention focused on the book she held open in her hands. Rafe took in the haphazard pile of books at her feet, and another two balanced precariously on the arm of the chair, with a feeling he could not quite place washing over him. It looked as if she'd been here for the whole of the two weeks they'd been in Scotland—two weeks in which he'd seen remarkably little of her.

But it was the expression on her face that made him stand so still for a moment, as if he had never seen her before. Perhaps he hadn't. She looked so…rapt. Engrossed. Unguarded. Filled with something he might have called wonder, if he still believed in such things. It made something deep within him stir to life, as if in recognition.

It was as if, he thought, she was an entirely different person than the one she'd so far showed him.

But then she looked up, and in that moment, that quickly, the Angel he knew slid into place across her face. That quick smile, those clever eyes, sizing him up in the space of a single breath. Weighing, measuring. She closed the book she was reading on a finger, and let that hand hang over the side of the chair, the book dangling. She met his gaze, her blue eyes clear. Open. He found he didn't believe it any longer.

"Is this where you've been hiding then?" he asked, his voice not nearly as calm as he would have preferred it. He expected her smile, but even so, the power of it moved through him like the wind. "For two weeks?"

"Has it been that long?" Her tone was dry. "As promised, the pleasures of the country are vast indeed. I didn't even notice."

"You have been nowhere to be found," he pointed out, fascinated to hear something more than polite inquiry in his own voice. How novel. "Are you hiding, Angel?"

"Of course not." Her eyebrows arched, her blue eyes that unreadable, darker hue as they met his. "Do I have something to hide from?"

Rafe moved further into the room, enjoying the way her gaze tracked his movements as if she couldn't help herself, and taking far too much satisfaction in the convulsive little swallow that moved in the column of her throat. He stopped when he reached her chair, then bent down to pick up the book that lay nearest him on the wide leather arm. He glanced at the title—a selection of poems from

the Elizabethan age—and set it back down, oddly discon-
certed.

"I did not realize you were such a great reader," he said.

It surprised him to find her here. It had been the last
place he'd looked when, today, he'd finally decided to go
searching through the rambling old house for some sign
of her. He couldn't say why he still felt as if it didn't make
sense that she should be here. Or why she looked entirely
too bland and innocent, as if he'd caught her at something
she shouldn't have been doing.

"I am attempting to figure out who you are through your
library," she said in her breezy way. She set down the book
she'd been reading and waved lazily at the nearest wall,
where shelves ran floor to ceiling and were packed with all
kinds of books, of different shapes and sizes, a controlled
chaos of words in, Rafe knew, at least six languages. He
had vowed he would read them all, one day. By his reck-
oning he was very nearly halfway through.

"By my books you will know me?" he asked quietly, his
gaze moving over the familiar shelves, seeing the spines
of books he had pored over, and others he was still waiting to discover.

She smiled as she always did, but her eyes were wary
when he looked at her again. "Something like that. Can
you be found here, do you think? Are your secrets hidden
between the pages somewhere?"

Rafe thrust his hands into his pockets as that wild desire for her spiked inside of him, hard and hot. It was that
or put them on her—sink his fingers into that wild, recal-
citrant hair all choppy about her face, run his hands over
the curves that were perfectly visible no matter that she sat
curled around herself—and he was sure that if he started
down that road, he would not stop. Perhaps not ever.

"This library was a particular passion of my grandfather's," he said instead, frowning at the wall of books before him, where ragged paperback volumes stood next to extraordinary editions of books long out of print, with early editions of well-known classics on the other side. "He believed that reading was the point, not the collection itself, which was considered a fairly revolutionary viewpoint at the time." He eyed her then. "If you locate any secrets in these books, I imagine they will be my grandfather's."

"I just like to read," she said in an odd sort of voice, as if, he realized slowly, she was offering her confession. "Anything and everything. I always have."

Angel unfolded herself from the chair, coming to her feet and then onto her toes, stretching in a way that made Rafe tense—and then harden even further as desire swamped him. As if she had been designed to test him she threw her arms over her head, her breasts jutting out, her back making a mouthwatering arc. She was dressed much like he was, in denim jeans and a jumper to keep off the chill of spring in this drafty old house, but the jumper she'd chosen seemed to lick over her curves, begging him to touch, to taste—

She was torturing him. And she wasn't even trying.

He knew better than to *want*. Especially like this. Especially this woman, who was not here for this, for him. Why couldn't he remember that? Why had he spent these past two weeks fighting the urge to possess her as if she would ever really be his in that way? As if he would ever allow it?

This was the wife he had bought, he reminded himself with a certain ruthless impatience. Even if—when—he did take her to his bed, how would he know which of her responses were real and which he'd purchased? He wouldn't. He couldn't. And instead of that sickening him as it should, Rafe found that the longer this woman was in his life—

under his roof—the less he cared why or how she came to his bed. He only cared about *when*.

He was such a fool.

"What if this had all burned down with the rest?" she was asking, unaware of his thoughts, pivoting where she stood to take in the rest of the great room, his grandfather's grand folly. The massive globe sat in the center of the library, requiring two hands to move it if one wished to peer at the map of a world that was no more, lost to time and the ravages of history, nations fallen and lands reclaimed, reconquered. A relic. A throwback. Not unlike its current owner. "I can't imagine losing so many books. I have only a few, really, but I treasure them."

"Luckily, this room never held much appeal for my brother," Rafe said dryly. It was an understatement—and it was why this had always been his refuge. Maybe that was why he felt unsettled by her presence here. It was, in many ways, his sanctuary. He felt her gaze on him, but when he turned to her, she was studying the books again. "He was the one who burned down the east wing," he continued gruffly. "Had he done so deliberately, he might very well have used the books as kindling, but it was an accident."

"I'm so sorry," she said after a moment. Too long a moment. Rafe sighed.

"Don't be." He couldn't imagine why he was discussing this. But he kept going, for reasons he could not fathom. "Oliver was remarkably unpleasant, even when he was a boy. It was not enough that he was the heir, he wanted to be the only child as well. He went to particular lengths to right what he saw as the great wrong of my birth." He let out a sound that even he knew was far too dark to be a laugh. "And that was when my father was still alive, and in control. And long before Oliver started drinking and became truly nasty."

Why was he telling her this? And why not tell her the real truth—that had taken all these years and Oliver's death for Rafe to accept? That there had to be a reason that Oliver treated Rafe the way he had, a reason that their mother had encouraged it. There had to be something in him that brought that kind of meanness out in them. He had been ruined even when he was a boy. But he couldn't bring himself to tell Angel that. He couldn't bear for her to know that particular truth.

"What did he do?" she asked, tilting her head slightly as she looked at him.

"I beg your pardon?"

"Everyone likes to claim they were picked on by their older siblings, don't they?" she asked in that deliberately offhand way of hers that made him feel lighter, no matter the subject. Even this one, which he had never found even remotely light. "Everyone loves to make themselves the martyr of their own story. And some people may be, of course. But there are others who think a single scuffle for the last biscuit one summer when they were eleven is more than enough justification for a lifetime of excuses."

She eyed him then, as if she expected him to confess to exactly that, and once again he found himself fighting the urge to laugh. It was unexpected and as shocking to him as the fact he'd told her anything about Oliver in the first place.

"Sadly," he said, his voice low, more to disguise his reaction to her than any indication of a matching mood, "Oliver was not the sort to scuffle for a biscuit. That would have been too straightforward. He preferred to mask his worst traits from any kind of parental eye and strike when least expected."

Angel eased herself back down to the chair, this time to perch herself on the empty arm, giving Rafe ample opportunity to wonder what had come over him. He'd had fevers that had affected him less than this woman. Whole wars, in fact.

"That's a bit like my mother then," she said. A strange expression moved over her lovely features, obscuring them for a moment. It was not until it was gone that Rafe realized what it was, why he recognized it even before he identified it. *Pain.* He knew it all too well. "She's always neck-deep in a scheme, and it's never what you think she'll do—never quite what she's done before. Though, inevitably, it will cost you. It always does, one way or another."

Something moved in the air between them, heavy and bright. Rafe felt his need for her like a pulse, coursing through him like blood. Only thicker. Sweeter. Hotter.

"Did your mother burn your house to the ground?" he asked. He didn't entirely understand the rueful expression that crossed her face then, much less the flash of something far sharper than amusement in her gaze.

"In a manner of speaking," she said, her lips moving into something a shade too serious to be a smile. "But there is no scaffolding to repair the sort of damage my mother can do, I'm afraid. She defies any attempt to rebuild."

"While the scaffolding cannot do a thing to keep the ghosts of Pembroke Manor at bay," he replied, something very near wry. "They merely wait their turn."

"The ghosts will always lie in wait, won't they?" Angel asked softly, her blue eyes dark on his. "We are all haunted in one way or another. This house. You. Me."

He did not want her wisdom, he realized then. Nor her understanding. It cut too deep. Whatever it was that arced between them pulled taut, clawing into him, making him completely unable to do anything but focus on her mouth. That wicked, taunting mouth. He welcomed it.

"What are you doing?" she asked, but her voice was no

more than the faintest whisper of sound. She stood again, as if to put distance between them, as if she meant to move to safer ground—but she didn't go anywhere. And now they were both standing, so close—*so close*—that he could easily reach over and—

"You know very well what I'm doing," he said, his voice far more of a growl than it should have been. Want and need pounded in him, making him so hard it bordered on pain. But he didn't touch her. He had promised her he would wait, hadn't he? And there was very little left of the man he should have been, he knew that. But he still had his word. There were times he thought it was all he had.

"Rafe…"

Again, that hard swallow, as if she was fighting the same demons and desires that he was, and with as much success.

"You have been hiding in this library for two weeks," he said, managing to keep his voice even, though he felt nothing at all but heat. "And I've let you. I wanted your transition to Pembroke Manor—to Scotland—to be as easy as possible." She only watched him, eyes wide and wary. And that shimmer of heat beneath, that called to him in ways he refused to explore. Not here. Not yet. "I have very few requirements, Angel," he continued. "But I would like you to have dinner with me in the evenings. Do you think you can do that?"

He was sure she could tell how much he wanted it—how he wanted *her*—and he wasn't sure who he hated more in that moment. Her, for being such a temptation that he made himself into a fool for her? Or himself, for being that fool? He did not know what he would do if he saw pity in her eyes, or worse, some kind of understanding—but that was not the expression that dawned there, and gleamed softly.

"Do we dress for dinner here?" she asked in her easy, offhanded way, as if she hadn't noticed all these currents swimming around them, all the tension simmering in the air.

"If you like." He shrugged, arousal making his voice as hard as the rest of him. "I cannot be bothered."

"I expected the role of countess to require far more gowns," she said, her tone reproving, as if she believed the matter of her wardrobe to be of paramount importance here, where there were only the two of them and a staff well paid to notice nothing at all. "If I may lodge a complaint."

"You may wear whatever you please," he said.

Maybe his voice was too rough. Maybe that was why she seemed to stiffen—but no, she only nodded, and he had the frustrating realization that she was hiding her true feelings, whatever they were, behind that amiable surface.

Again.

As usual.

He hated that too.

"Except," he said, and there was no doubting his voice was too rough now, too rough and too hard, like the monster she kept making him forget he was, forcing him to wonder if she considered that service simply part of the bargain—part of the price he'd paid. "That mask you wear all the time. I'd prefer you leave that in your room. If at all possible."

His words hung in her mind as Angel swept into the small, intimate dining room later that same evening, dressed in the finest gown she'd been able to find among her belongings—all of it carefully unpacked and painstakingly hung in the extensive closets in her rooms by unseen if capable hands. It was a deliberately extravagant dress of deepest crimson that flowed over her body from a bold, asymmetrical neckline to pool at her feet like a living, breathing flame. She knew it made her look as if she were planning to make herself the main course—to incinerate them both with the force of her brightness.

She was hoping it would distract Rafe from this talk of masks. After all, the mask she wore—the easy, happy mask she *had* to wear with him—was the only thing she had that was hers. The only thing she had left.

The only thing she hadn't signed away.

"Good evening, my lord," she said with greatly exaggerated courtesy, and had to fight to restrain herself from sketching a theatrical curtsy in his direction.

"My lady," he murmured in cool reply, in a manner that made Angel question her own sanity—and her seeming need to poke at this man as if he were a tiger locked up in a cage. She had no trouble imagining him in the role of a big cat, all sinew and grace, danger in every solid inch of his sleekly muscled body. But she'd do well to remember the only one in any sort of cage around here, gilded or not, was her.

He loomed there beside the long, narrow table against the far wall, much too dark and menacing for what was meant to be a cozier dining room than the formal hall in this great house, and what was frightening wasn't that she found him scary—but that she did not. Quite the opposite. She had thought him far too compelling, far too *much,* in his fine Italian suits, all elegant lines and inspired tailoring—none of which he wore tonight. As he had promised, he did not dress for dinner.

He didn't have to.

Rafe in a simple pair of denim jeans and a sleek dark navy jumper almost did her in. His hair was too long, and bore the marks of impatient hands run through the thick, dark locks. He was too grim, too hard, too impossibly male. When he wore a suit, he was so obviously *the earl*—distant and dangerous, but quite clearly out of reach in every way that mattered. Here, now, dressed so casually, he was only a man. But what a man! It was as if she could *see* all that power and shattering sensuality coiled and ready in his distractingly masculine form. *Waiting.* It made her throat go dry, even as the rest of her softened, melted, ached.

Her reaction to him terrified her far more than he did.

"You are staring," he pointed out, and there was something in his voice that seemed to skitter over her skin like a kind of touch. She had to force herself to breathe.

"I am trying to find the earl in this particular costume," she said, sweeping her gaze over him from his carelessly tousled head to the feet he'd encased in hard black boots. He should have looked far less magnificent than he did. He should have faded into mediocrity without the fine clothes that marked him as the wealthy, powerful man he was. But Angel looked at the way he stood there, so easy and confident, and knew that whatever this man was, he didn't need clothes to broadcast it. He simply exuded it from his very pores.

That should have made her nervous, surely. She told herself it did, that *nerves* explained the jumpy, achy feeling low in her belly.

"I was the earl long before I had any hope of the title," he said, in a voice that hinted at secrets and stories she doubted he would share. "I suspect it is in me whether I like it or not, clothes be damned. It is like the family curse."

He was so dark, so serious, with his soldier's stance and his ravaged face, and yet she had the nearly overwhelming urge to close the distance between them and see if she could taste the white-hot heat of him on his tongue. He was magnetic and fascinating, and how, she wondered with something like despair, could she handle this marriage of hers if she was no better than a moth to the nearest bright light? If she had the suicidal urge to simply throw herself at him and see what became of her?

He studied her for a moment, his gray eyes cold, and she had the sinking sensation that he could read every single thought that crossed her mind. As if he knew exactly what effect he had on her. As if he was luring her in with every breath, every near-smile. *Don't be ridiculous,* she chided herself. *He is only a man.* Two weeks in Scotland and she'd gone over all gothic, apparently. Next thing she knew she'd be waxing rhapsodic about the joys of sheep.

She accepted the glass of wine he handed her, and their fingers brushed as she took it. Such a small, silly thing, hardly worth noticing—and yet her heart stuttered, then began to beat harder, like a drum.

"You spoke of requirements earlier," she said, determined that her voice should not sound as breathless as she felt. She forced some facsimile of her usual easy smile, unable to control herself as she should. "Perhaps you should list them all for me, so there is no further confusion."

"I am not in the least confused," he replied smoothly, a small quirk in the corner of his mouth that she took to be his version of a smile. "But then, I am not the one who worried that the countryside would affect her sanity."

"I have been in it very little, as it turns out," Angel replied, still smiling at him. As if it were her job. Which, she reflected with a pang, it was. "From inside the house, if I squint, I can pretend I'm near enough to London."

"I admire your dedication to remaining in your fantasy world," he said dryly. "I'm sure it will serve you well here."

That didn't sit well with her, but she couldn't address it even if she'd known how, because he was moving toward a chair and pulling it out for her. He settled her into it with a certain ease that made her feel too warm, then took the chair opposite hers, and nodded at one of the hovering, silent servants.

Dinner was a long, strange affair. Course after course appeared, each more succulent and delicious than the one before. They ate, they talked. Angel kept the conversation going, poking fun at him as much as she dared, making his gray eyes warm just slightly from time to time. She told silly stories from her many different lives, embroidering each one, dramatizing them. She felt like some modern-day version of Scheherazade, spinning tales to keep herself alive, though she couldn't have said what she thought the threat was, here. Or what the price might be if she stopped.

Until the final plate was cleared away, and there were only the candles in their gleaming silver holders between them, the flames dancing in the sudden, airless silence.

"Have you run out of stories to tell?" Rafe asked, his voice very nearly lazy. He had relaxed his posture over the course of the meal, and now lounged in his chair, his hand propping up his chin, his face half-shadowed. In the candlelight, Angel realized with a certain shock, she could see none of his scars—only his hard, male beauty.

That, then, was the price.

She was in so much trouble.

"Of course not," she said, aware that her voice was too soft, too pliable, telling him things she was not at all sure she wanted him to know. "I feel perfectly capable of at least a thousand and one nights of stories. Possibly twice that. You can consider it my wedding gift to you."

He only watched her. Angel was no fool. She knew exactly what hovered in the air then, what seemed to dance between them, making each breath feel thick, dangerous. And there was no denying the fact that she wanted him, however suicidally. He fascinated her. That darkness that moved in him, that cast him into shadows, was far more compelling to her than it should have been. She wanted to touch it. Him. She wanted to let herself fall forward into the swirl of these feelings, this tension, and who cared where she landed?

But she could not let herself do it. She was far too afraid of where she might end up, and what falling in the first place would make her.

Like mother, like daughter, that little voice whispered.

"I think that is my cue to go up to bed," she said quietly, her voice seeming twice as loud now in the hush of the small room, in the unwavering, patient heat of his dark gaze. "I have a very busy day of doing very little ahead of me, and must conserve my strength."

"Allow me," he said in that silky way of his that seemed to hit her hard, low in her belly, and tight across the crest of her breasts. He rose, his every move somehow fluid, all that repressed power making him something near graceful despite his size and strength. And Angel could do nothing but gaze at him, entranced, as he moved around the table to pull out her chair, the very picture of gentlemanly courtesy despite his casual clothes.

It was so much harder than it should have been to stand, to step away from him, when every cell in her body screamed for her to move toward him instead. To press her lips to that fascinating place where the strong column of his throat met his chest. It took more strength than it should have to turn from him and walk toward the door.

She thought she might have hurt herself somehow—tearing herself away like this—but she did it anyway, because she had to ignore this wild passion that burned so hot between them. She had to—or it would eat her alive. She knew it. She'd seen what happened to those who surrendered to this kind of heat, and she wouldn't do that to herself. She couldn't.

"Angel."

She stopped without knowing she meant to do so, her body obeying him without consulting her mind. She swayed slightly on her feet, and put out her hand to the doorjamb to steady herself. She did not turn back around. She was much too afraid of what would happen if she did.

Liar, that same voice chided her. *You know what would happen. And you're not afraid at all.*

Not of this moment, perhaps, she admitted to herself. But of what would come after.

She sensed him more than she heard him come up behind her, and she began to tremble just slightly in helpless reaction, but she still did not turn to face him. He moved closer, until his legs brushed the back of her full skirt and she felt the whisper-soft wool of his jumper brush against the bare skin near her exposed shoulder blades. Did she feel the heat of him, burning like a furnace in the cool room, or did she imagine it?

Did it matter? The effect on her was the same.

"Rafe—" she began.

"Quiet." It was a command, for all that he said it softly, his breath caressing the back of her neck, making gooseflesh prickle into life all over her skin.

He reached around and let his fingers run down the arm that hung at her side, spreading a sweet, heavy fire into her with his touch, making her whole body seem to tremble, there, on the precipice between panic and desire. Both, perhaps. He took her free hand in his, then raised it, bringing it up and placing it on the opposite side of the door, so she was bracing herself in the doorway, splayed open before him. Her fingers clutched convulsively against the plaster. Why would he...?

And that was when he moved even closer, until his body was flush against hers, plastering her back against his strong, impossibly hard chest. Angel heard herself sigh, and felt herself melt. Everywhere. Her head fell back against his shoulder, as if she had lost the will to keep herself upright. He muttered something, his voice rich and dark, even as her hands clung to the doorjamb as if it was her only link to any kind of safety. As if she could hold herself there— apart. As if that could protect her from this. From him.

From herself.

He leaned down then and pressed his mouth, open and hot, to that exquisitely tender place just below her ear.

And Angel went up in flames.

CHAPTER SEVEN

It was like lightning—jagged and bright, coursing through her, into her.

Angel heard herself whimper, and then he was taking her mouth with his, still holding her so her back was to him, his kiss wild. Unmanageable. Impossible to resist.

She didn't try. She kissed him back with all of her uncertainty, her fascination. All of the want and need she'd been trying to pretend she didn't feel. This was not the stamp of possession, brief and encompassing, that had marked the occasion of their marriage. This was not even that far more dangerous kiss they'd shared on the dance floor of the Palazzo Santina. This kiss was changing her, somehow. Making her his.

Angel understood on some primal level that Rafe had been holding himself in check before. That he still was, even as his mouth moved against hers with a devastating thoroughness; even as he took her mouth again and again until she was frantic with the taste of him and desperate for more.

His hands moved, tracing their way down her sides, following the artful fall of the shimmering crimson that sheathed her. Then back up again, until his hard palms found her breasts and tested their shape and fullness, making her writhe against him. She felt the heat of him behind her, the hard press of his powerful body, and then, more than that, she felt the unmistakable thrust of his arousal against her bottom.

It made her feel weak. Wild. Capable of anything and everything to get even closer to him. She tried to turn, but he did not allow it, and she found her nails digging into the doorjamb again as his hands moved lower, pulling up the heavy skirt she wore and investigating beneath.

"Rafe…" she managed to say when he pulled his mouth from hers, only to lick a path of wildfire down the length of her neck. "Rafe, I…"

She didn't know what she meant to say.

"Hold on," he said, his voice a dark and heavy magic behind her, as one hand smoothed its way along her leg, then onto her thigh, making her breath come too fast, her knees turn to water.

"Hold on?" she echoed, not comprehending him, not capable of thought when he was touching her like this, his palm so hot against her skin, his hard fingers faintly rough, as if calloused—and then his clever fingers found the tiny thong she wore, in a matching, wicked red.

Her fingers clutched at the door.

"Hold on…" she breathed.

She thought he laughed, which should have been impossible, and then he was moving beneath the tiny scrap of fabric and holding the heat of her in his hard palm. He traced a lazy pattern there, and Angel moaned, moving with him, her head falling back against him, her eyes drifting closed. Her hips moved of their own accord, chasing those teasing, tormenting fingers, until he shifted slightly and thrust into her slick heat.

One long finger, then another, and Angel forgot how to breathe.

He set the pace, and she met it. She rode his hand, chasing that wildfire, more and more desperate with each rolling thrust of his fingers. She was aware of the other arm that wrapped around her waist and held her tight against his body, and that hard, serious mouth that continued to taste her, drinking in the sounds she made, encouraging every sigh and whimper and moan. Sensation built on sensation until she was nothing at all but lost in the feel of him, the wild perfection of it, the agony and glory of this man and the way he played her body like an instrument made only for him, only for this—

And then she shattered in his hands like glass.

When she came back to herself he had let her skirt drop back down to the floor, though he continued to stand there, so still and strong behind her. Her legs were so shaky beneath her that she was not at all certain they would hold her. She shifted, dropping her hands and turning, sinking against the door as she finally faced him.

It was like a punch in the gut, hard and sharp. He was too fierce, too focused. He could see far too much. Once again, she was aware of his scars only after she'd absorbed the impact of his cold gaze, his dangerous expression, and even then, they only seemed to underscore what she knew about him. What she'd just experienced. That he was entirely too powerful here. That he could make her do anything, and she would enjoy it.

More than enjoy it.

His dark eyes glittered in the shadows of the room, and she was sure she could hear the echoes of her cries rebounding from the high walls. She felt some emotion she couldn't name move through her then, shaking her. She was afraid to name it—afraid to face it.

He reached up a hand to touch her cheek, his face so very fierce, his gaze so hard, so relentless, and she could not handle the intensity. She could not allow herself to feel this way. She could not allow herself to *feel*. But the emotion seemed to swell in her, tightening and sharpening, and she balked at the feel of his hard palm against her skin, balked at the sheer possessiveness in even so small a gesture.

It was slight—she hardly moved a muscle—but he froze.

"Ah, yes," he said, his voice harsh in the quiet of the room. Bitter condemnation and severe judgment warred on his grim face, while that flash of near silver in his dark eyes that looked too much like pain nearly made her weep. "It is so much less exciting when you must look the monster in the eye, isn't it? Impossible to pretend it is someone else touching you—someone less hideous to look upon, for a start. My apologies. I lost my head."

She thought she said his name, but he didn't look at her again.

He moved past her in the doorway, and then disappeared into the darkness of the manor house, leaving Angel to cling to the door as if it might keep her from falling while her heart pounded out a sickening beat in her chest and she wondered what, exactly, she'd just lost.

Angel could not sleep.

She'd tried everything to get herself to drift off into slumber, and had failed. She'd counted sodding sheep, but that had only made her more agitated. She'd attempted to quiet her mind—with precious little success. She'd even started to write a long, detailed e-mail to Allegra, her princess bride of a stepsister, but she'd given up several long and twisted paragraphs into all the tortured back story that had led her to this night and everything that had happened.

Sensible, play-it-safe Allegra was not likely to understand the things that had compelled Angel to marry Rafe, much less the things that Angel could hardly bear to express about what had passed between them without any words at all. So how could Angel possibly explain to her the potent mix of despair and deep, encompassing delight that coursed through her even hours later, marking her like some kind of internal tattoo, making her think she would die if Rafe put his hands on her again?

Or worse, she thought in some moments, if he did not?

That, Angel had decided, was far too much to dump in an email to her stepsister, who was probably carried aloft by doves and rainbows nightly with the force of her royal love, or something equally unimaginable and over-the-top, as suited the soon-to-be Princess of Santina. If she'd wanted Allegra's counsel and input, she should have included her in this madness from the start, before things grew so wholly out of control. But she had not. She had—as ever—completely failed to imagine any circumstance in which she might need someone else, even as a friend to reach out to on a dark night when she suspected she'd acted terribly and foolishly, and so she was now forced to rely on only herself.

As usual.

Have found myself stranded in the middle of Scottish countryside, of all places, with only an earl (quite attractively wealthy) and a rambling old house (crumbling all around us as I type, sadly) for entertainment, she'd written, knowing it would make Allegra smile to imagine Angel in such circumstances, so far from her usual London stomping grounds, much less any hope of a quick Tube ride to somewhere more exciting. Would give you the address, but am slightly afraid I've been transported to medieval times and will at any moment be expected to don a corset or some other form of fancy dress. (A wimple? The mind boggles!) The good news is that I have yet to see a kilt, hear a bagpipe or taste anything too horrible like haggis, but suspect all of the above lurk in my near future. Kilts and bagpipes I might manage to survive but haggis? A fate worse than death! Hope all is well with Prince Charming. Xx

It might not have been what Angel had really wanted to write, but it helped for a while after she hit Send and closed her laptop back up. It was the reaching out, perhaps, that made her feel less alone, no matter the form it took. But it didn't last.

The dawn was little more than a pale blue yearning outside her windows when Angel gave up, and swung her feet to the cold floor. There was a scooped-out, empty feeling inside of her, and it had only grown worse as the hours passed. She'd tortured herself with images of Rafe. His clever hands, his wicked fingers. His cruel, delicious mouth, so demanding against hers, so patient and knowing.

And that frozen look in his eyes when he'd thought she'd rejected him. Did he think it was his scars? She wished, with a part of herself she was not at all proud of, that it was that simple. That she was that shallow. She imagined that would be easier, somehow.

The truth was, Angel admitted to herself with a surge of that same old panic, she wasn't cut out for this. Not any of it. She'd had no idea how difficult it would be to *actually* marry for money—to attempt to forge a relationship out of nothing but mercenary urges and a stack of signed contracts. She might be forced to consider Chantelle in a whole new light, as whatever her mother's sins, she had somehow managed to maintain a marriage based on nothing more than a shared lust for Bobby's fame and fortune for all these years. But Angel wasn't her mother, no matter the surface similarities. She couldn't be, because she knew all too well that Chantelle had never had a moment's bit of trouble with her choices in life, and this was *killing* Angel a scant two weeks into it.

She wanted too much, for one thing. She wanted Rafe to talk to her, to smile at her. Why did she want that so badly—so very badly that it was rapidly becoming an obsession? She wanted him to think well of her, to share all those murky secrets she could sense swirling around inside of him like dark shadows. She wanted him to *like* her— how crazy was that? She *wanted,* and she did not need to consult the international handbook of appropriate behavior for trophy wives, should such a thing exist outside of certain deeply appalling American television programs, to understand that that was only likely to get her into trouble. To muddy things and confuse the issue.

What was wrong with maintaining a healthy, polite distance in her marriage of convenience? Why wasn't that enough for her?

And that, of course, was all completely apart from the real issue, which was this deadly, sensual fascination with her husband, the man. This…driving need for him that she could hardly understand. Even now, hours later, she had only to think of him and her body shivered into readiness. Into sensual urgency. Her core melted. Her breasts grew heavy. And the impossible heat that swirled through her, coiling between her legs, made her want to scream. Cry. *Something.*

No, she ordered herself, horrified at how close she'd come to losing herself here. Already. *No tears.*

This was all a mistake. All of it. She should have listened to her own gut when she'd had the chance. Now she was embroiled in something she couldn't understand, that made her *feel* the kinds of things she'd always vowed to herself she'd never be so foolish as to feel—out of control, off-balance, half-mad over some man. Over *her husband.*

She simply couldn't take it.

It was easy enough to pull on her clothes—her favorite pair of jeans, a long-sleeved T-shirt and a heavy jumper to ward off the cold, damp morning. She pulled on a pair of low-heeled boots, wrapped a bright scarf around her neck and stuck her wallet in her back pocket—more for identification purposes than any kind of access to funds. She didn't need anything else. She didn't need anything she'd had before, or anything that was his. What she needed most of all was to escape—to find something, somewhere, that could be hers and hers alone. As usual. As ever.

She crept out of the countess's ornate chamber that felt no more like hers than it had when she'd arrived and headed for the front door, aware for the first time how the fine old manor creaked and settled around her, as if it really did house a fleet of madwomen-turned-ghosts in its drafty halls. She had no trouble believing it. It wasn't even particularly difficult to imagine herself turning into one of them, creeping about in the shadows of Rafe's manor, a phantom even to herself. The image made her shudder.

It was lighter outside when she stepped out into the cold morning, the sky a gunmetal gray that lightened almost imperceptibly by the moment, heralding the approach of the sun.

And she walked. And walked, taking deep breaths in the chilly dawn, pulling the sharp, cold air as far into her as it could go before blowing it out in big clouds.

She was not running away, she told herself as her feet crunched through the glittering frost that spread across the long, winding, picturesque drive that she knew led to a road that in turn led to a village…eventually. She was regrouping. Rethinking.

Because the only thing she could think of that was worse than being forever in Chantelle's clutches, subject to her whims and schemes, was…this. This hollow, desperate feeling. This impossible, driving need. This wild, chaotic, out of control madness that she was entirely too afraid would take over her life, if she let it.

She worried it already had.

She knew where this kind of thing led. She was the walking, talking result of it, wasn't she? Chantelle had never let Angel forget that in her long career of finding the right men to take her all the places she wanted to go, simply because she asked them to, Chantelle had truly fallen for one of them exactly once.

"Lose your head, love, and you lose control," her mother had told her more times than she could count, usually to the accompaniment of sloppy cigarette smoke circles blown in the air. "And then you lose everything, don't you?"

"I will never be you," Angel had told her mother once, very seriously, when she couldn't have been more than nine years old and Chantelle had been beating that familiar drum, as she liked to do when feeling maudlin—usually brought on by being a bit too far into her cups.

Chantelle had only laughed that time. "That's what they all say," she'd retorted. "But none of us are so high and mighty that love can't cut us down to size, Angel. Even me." Angel could remember her derisive snort with perfect clarity. "Even you."

But Angel had been deadly serious.

She'd never met her father. She never wanted to meet him. Any married man who got a teenaged girl pregnant and then promptly abandoned her was no one Angel needed to know, thank you very much. But it was the fact that Chantelle—street-smart and canny Chantelle, who had never met a man she couldn't sweet talk into doing things her way—had lost her head over him in the first place that had truly scared her. She'd fallen hard for him, Chantelle had told Angel ruefully every time the subject had come up, and then he'd been the one calling all the shots. For the first and last time.

If that was what that kind of heady, all-consuming passion did to you—made you that foolish, that gullible, that easily manipulated—then Angel wanted nothing to do with it. A personal mantra that had always served her well.

Until Rafe.

She was afraid of him, she realized as she made her lonely way down the long, rambling drive, dipping in and out of the dark woods and catching glimpses even she could admit were breathtaking of the loch with its glassy, still waters and the looming mountains beyond. She was afraid that this kind of shattering passion would ruin her, as surely as it had ruined her mother before her. She was afraid that if she truly succumbed to it, if she surrendered, she would never really be herself again.

And she had no one *but* herself. She was the one person she couldn't let herself lose.

She didn't know why she stopped walking. The drive had brought her almost to the banks of the loch, and she stared out moodily over the clear water. The mountains rose inexorably in the distance, blue and purple, and even though she knew better, even though she told herself it was silly and sentimental, she turned to look back the way she'd come, toward Pembroke Manor, which she could see perched there at the top of the hill she'd been slowly making her way down all this time.

She told herself she had no idea why that view, pretty though it might be, should make her whole body ache as if she'd suddenly caught some kind of virus. Bones, muscles, skin. It all hurt in a low, deep throb that she was afraid would never end.

Or was she more afraid that it would?

And now what? she asked herself, her eyes still fixed on the half-ruined manor, much like its master in that its ravaged wing in no way took away from its grace and beauty. The morning sun was just starting to shine upon it, making it glow slightly. *Where will you go? What will you do?*

She had no friends, not really, because she never let anyone close. Ever. She hardly thought her actual family members—silly, self-involved Izzy and their mercenary mother—qualified for the term, and the non–blood relations who did, like Allegra and Ben, she would never dream of disturbing with her real troubles. She'd already told Allegra more than she'd told Ben, and what had she really told either of them? Nothing that mattered. She admitted to herself that she didn't know how. Beyond that, she had no money—and would have even less should she once again owe that fifty thousand pounds. She had no useful qualifications, and was on the wrong end of her twenties to think that modeling gigs could continue to pay her rent. And thanks to Rafe and his efficient staff, she had no flat to return to anyway.

And the truth was, she accepted reluctantly as the cold morning sun shone above her, making all the turmoil rolling around inside of her seem simple, finally—none of that would have mattered if she'd really wanted to leave. She didn't. And that was the most terrifying part of it all.

She heard movement behind her and, when she turned, it was to see Rafe stepping out from the woods. She should have been surprised by that, but she wasn't. She doubted there was very much that slipped by this man in his own house, now that she considered it. Just as she wasn't surprised by the way her heart leaped in her chest, and started to beat just that little bit too fast as she let her gaze move over his guarded expression, his long, rangy body.

"I didn't take you for the sort who enjoyed a morning constitutional," Rafe said, his voice colder than the air around them as he moved toward her in that way of his that made her think of the word *prowling.* "As it involves the outdoors and the countryside."

He was even more closed off today than usual, Angel saw, shut down and remote, and she felt that deep sorrow for him reverberate within her chest, fusing with the *want* and the *need* and making a mockery of everything she'd told herself.

The truth was that she wanted him far more than she wanted to protect herself. When had that happened? But there it was.

"I'm opposed to it in principle and in fact," she agreed. She searched those stony eyes, looking for the Rafe she knew, but he was a cold, watchful stranger once again, hidden securely away behind that stiff soldier's stance and that grim mouth. And even so, he came close enough that she had to tilt her head back to look him in the eye. Close enough that she could have reached out and touched him, if she dared. She raised her eyebrows. "I was running away, obviously."

"So soon?" His voice was bitter, his eyes dark. But he did not sound at all surprised, which rankled more than it should. "I thought you were a bit more stubborn than that."

Angel smiled, though it felt thin. She wanted to touch him. She wanted to reach out and slide her hands beneath the black coat he'd thrown on over his usual uniform of casual jumper and jeans, to feel the heat of him. Even after everything that had happened, she wanted him.

Maybe, she thought in no little despair and as much panicked confusion, she always would. Maybe it had been too late for her from the start—from the moment she'd clapped eyes on him at that ball.

"It's lucky that you are possessed of a large estate," she said casually, as if there was nothing between them but some sparkling conversation. "My urge to run away disappeared in the time it might have taken me to hail a taxi. But all you seem to have here are ten thousand trees and views of the loch, so here I am. Plan thwarted."

He didn't respond to her lighter tone. He didn't crack even his bare-bones version of a smile. If anything, his gaze only darkened as he looked at her, and she had the distinct impression of barely leashed ferocity, burning off of him in waves.

"I can't think what could have put you over the edge," he bit out, his voice scathing, as if he could not manage to hold it back or keep it cool. "It must have been dire indeed, to launch you from your bed at so uncivilized an hour, and force you out into the depths of nature."

He was daring her, provoking her, and it made her hurt for him. For her. For this terrible situation between them—this cold-blooded marriage—that she knew, somehow, she could never fix. Could never, ever make right. Not really. Not for the first time, she wondered what might have become of them if she had never mentioned money when she'd met him. If he had never offered to be her savior. Where would they be now?

But that was one more thing she'd never know.

Something like a sob welled up within her, but she shoved it back down. She reached over and took his face in her hands before she could think better of it, letting her right palm caress the scars that swept over the left side of his gorgeous face, feeling it like a blow when he flinched. But she didn't move her hands, not even when he covered them with his own, as if he meant to pull hers away. His gray eyes gleamed a shade of silver she'd never seen before—*pain,* she thought, *that means he is in pain*—and she didn't look away.

"I saw you first," she said, knowing somehow that this was the greater vow, these quiet words in a chapel made of the woods and the water, with the watchful mountains in the distance. Whether he ever knew it or not. She did. "I saw your dark eyes and your quiet strength, and it took my breath away."

"You saw that I had the look of a wealthy man," he said, his voice clipped and cold. But there was an arrested sort of look in those dark eyes now, and he did not pull away. He did not break the connection.

"That too," Angel agreed, and it was the sad truth, wasn't it? She'd have to learn how to live with what that meant for them. And in any case, it didn't matter here. Now. She gazed up at him. She let herself feel all those huge and terrible things she refused to name. And she smiled at him, a real smile, one that tried to do nothing at all but smile.

No mask. Only the stark truth she had yet to admit to herself, written all over her face, whether he saw it or not. She could feel it. Transforming her. Leaving her more vulnerable to this man than she had ever been to anyone, and ever would.

It was dizzying. It was terrifying. But she kept going, spurred on by something that felt far bigger than her own terrors, her own fears.

"And it was only after that, Rafe," she whispered, his scars warm beneath her hand, and his own palm hot above it, her eyes glued to his and her face, her heart, wide open, "that I noticed that you were scarred."

For a taut stretch of time, glittering and breathless, they only gazed at each other, and then his grim mouth moved, curving into something as sad as it was bitter. His hands were warm against hers, his eyes so very cold. *Lonely,* she thought. It made her ache.

"Ah, Angel," he said, his voice hoarse, scratchy with all that pain she was afraid she'd never understand. Not really. Not if he wouldn't let her. "The scars are the least of it."

CHAPTER EIGHT

THEY settled into a pattern in the weeks that followed that shattering morning.

Rafe had only stared at her for a long while, the tension like a vice around them both, his hands clenching slightly around hers, as if he fought off demons she couldn't see in the air between them while his eyes ran the gamut from a dark, stormy gray to liquid silver. They had eventually returned to the manor house, Angel far more confused by her own behavior than she wanted to admit. She'd accepted how very little she really wanted to go anywhere. She'd had her chance, hadn't she? If Angel had been less practical, more sentimental, she might have been tempted to note that they seemed to be conducting a kind of courtship as the days slipped by and they danced their highly charged sort of attendance upon each other—on the wrong side of the altar, to be sure, but a kind of courtship all the same.

But she didn't think about that, and she certainly didn't think about what it all might mean, because *that,* she told herself firmly, would be truly mad, and what she was doing was…something else. Something she could not let herself name.

They ate together in the mornings in that same small dining room, which boasted tall, graceful windows overlooking the loch and the brooding mountains to the east, so that it filled with bright morning sunshine on fine mornings. Or, more properly, Rafe ate the sort of hearty breakfast Angel associated with farmers and laborers, while Angel tried not to think about the ungodliness of the hour as she fortified herself with huge, steaming mugs of the best coffee she'd ever tasted.

She stopped asking herself why she got up so early in the morning, simply to sit with this man as he prepared for his day, quite as if theirs was a real marriage in every respect. She discovered that she never really liked her answer. It was no more and no less than the coffee, she decided. She preferred that explanation.

"You look as if you have achieved some kind of religious ecstasy," Rafe said one morning in an odd voice, as if he was taken back. Angel started, and realized she'd let her eyes drift closed as she sipped at the aromatic, dark brew. She smiled at him, then directed her attention to the thick ceramic mug between her palms.

"I believe I have," she said with a happy sigh. "I think you must import this coffee directly from the heavens. There can be no other explanation."

"Kenya actually." He sat back in his chair and was, she realized belatedly, studying her, a gleam in his dark eyes that struck her as particularly, decidedly male. It made that ever-present heat flame anew within her, making her skin seem to shrink against her bones. "My great-grandfather bought a small coffee plantation there at the start of the last century. I've always thought the coffee magnificent, but I'm aware I'm biased."

Angel stared into her mug, willing her body to relax, to fight that fire that only ever burned hotter between them, and never went out entirely.

"It's never simple with you, is it?" she asked. "You've never just nipped down to the local coffee shop for their special blend and thrown it in a carafe like a normal person. It has to be from the family coffee plantation, in *Kenya* of all places, to be suitably exotic." But she smiled as she looked at him, her brows arching high. "Any other little details like that you've forgotten to tell me? A palace or two tucked away somewhere, hardly worth mentioning? A small chain of islands in the Caribbean? Anything?"

He didn't smile. Not this cold, hard man, not quite, but his grim mouth softened, and his dark eyes gleamed. "Nothing comes to mind."

"And why would it?" Angel asked, rolling her eyes. "I suppose it's all run of the mill to you. A plantation in Kenya, an estate in Scotland—all just a day in the life of Lord Pembroke. Very boring, I'm sure."

"I am never bored by my responsibilities," Rafe said in a tone that should have been quelling, and might have been, had that same gleam not still been lighting up his gaze. "Someday, perhaps, you can use that quick mind of yours to help me rather than simply sitting about the place making clever remarks."

"Perhaps I will," Angel said, not knowing how to take that. Not knowing what he meant. Did he have the same image she did then—of the two of them, working together toward a common purpose? *As if this is all real after all,* that irrepressible voice whispered inside of her.

He pushed his chair back from the table and stood, presenting her with an unobstructed view of that lean, hard body of his in all its tough, masculine glory and making her forget anything and everything else.

"I am partial to islands in the Caribbean," he said. "Excellent suggestion. I'll have to look into that."

Angel's mouth went dry. She took another pull from her mug to keep from choking on what she suspected was pure, unadulterated lust. She assured herself that it was the prospect of whole Caribbean islands at her disposal, but she knew better.

It was Rafe. It was always Rafe.

He was wearing jeans, as usual, which hung low on his hips and clung to his perfect backside and meant he planned to labor alongside the construction team that came daily to work on the ruined wing of the house. Today he wore a rugged-looking button-down shirt, rolled up at the cuffs. There was absolutely nothing about this very casual, unremarkable ensemble that should have made Angel's heart flutter wildly, and yet it did.

Oh, it did.

She meant to keep the easy, breezy chatter going, to continue in her unofficial role as ambassador of good cheer in this marriage, the better to balance his eternal grimness, but she couldn't seem to manage it in that moment. Rafe took a last gulp of his own coffee, then set it back on the table, all seemingly casual—and yet his dark eyes seemed to be alive with *that heat*. That insidious, impossible heat. It burned away inside of her, eating her whole from within.

She remembered her hands on his face in the woods, his skin so hot in the cold air, his scars under one palm and the rasp of his beard-roughened jaw beneath the other. That same look in his eyes as the world seemed to shatter all around them. He'd taken her breath away then. He was doing it now.

His mouth crooked slightly in the corner. She wanted him to put his hands on her, his mouth—anything....

"I told you I wouldn't touch you again," he said, his voice like silk, low and addictive. "Did I not?"

"You did." Angel hardly recognized her own voice, had to blink away the heat glazing over her eyes. "What was it? Ah, yes. A stated concern for my tender sensibilities, despite my clear indication that I have none that should concern you."

He had been so faultlessly polite, so relentlessly formal, that night after she'd failed so spectacularly to leave him, and they'd sat once more over a meal fraught with all the things neither one of them could say out loud. He'd apologized for what he'd called "the scene" between them, and then he'd assured her that it would not happen again.

"Unless and until you want it to happen," he'd said, his low, gruff voice promising her everything she wanted and yet was afraid to ask for. Sex. Heat. Her surrender. His command. And then more of the same.

All with that same bright fire in his gaze. That challenge.

"If that is so," he replied now, his dark gray eyes nearly pewter, and polished to a high shine that made a kind of chill sneak over her skin, "then you need only say the word."

He was so deliciously male, so clearly, entrancingly dangerous. She could feel the force of him, the power, moving through her body, using it against her, making her *want*. Making her *need*. Making her think, in moments like this, that she might go mad if she didn't taste him again. That it might kill her if she did.

His voice dipped lower as his dark eyes moved over her the way she wished his hands would. "Any word."

They kept having this conversation.

And Angel didn't know why she didn't do what every part of her body longed for her to do, and had wanted since that morning in the woods—since the night that had precipitated it, and even before that, if she was honest. She didn't know why she didn't simply rise from her seat and close the distance between them, letting the morning sun spill all around them as she put an end to this dangerous, torturous game. She already knew how those strong, tough hands would feel against her skin. She had spent long nights keeping herself awake and aching with memories of his talented, wicked mouth, so hard and commanding against hers.

She knew exactly what she was missing.

But still, she did nothing. One long, hot moment turned into another. She only returned that simmering, stirring gaze of his, and then, somehow, smiled. The way she always did, coward that it turned out she was.

"Fair enough," he said as if she'd amused him yet again, as if his patience was boundless—or he was just supremely, arrogantly certain about how this would end—and then he left the room. Just as he always did.

It was only then that she let herself breathe.

And admit the truth. She knew that it was only a matter of time before she surrendered to this wild heat between them. To him. She could feel that clock ticking with every beat of her heart. And she knew, somehow, that once she did she would never be the same again. It was foolish, perhaps, but there it was. Rafe was too potent, too overpowering. And her impossible, highly unsuitable feelings for him had already inspired her to act completely out of character, more than once. She was already too weak where he was concerned. Too fascinated. Too spellbound. Too in awe.

Making love to him would be, she was sure, the worst mistake of a life already littered quite liberally with them. It would stand as a dividing line between *before* and *after,* and she had no way to know, now, what parts of herself she would give up in the process of crossing that line. She only knew that it would cost her to do it. No doubt dearly.

Not that that would stop her, she thought then, her mouth twisting into something wry as she brought her coffee back to up to her lips and took another transformative sip, wishing he were as easy to sink into as the coffee he served. As uncomplicated. But as long as she could make herself wait, she would—and pretend that she still had some tiny bit of control in this marriage, some tiny bit of power.

Because she knew, deep inside, with a kind of feminine intuition that she'd never experienced before and which shook her to the bone with its own inexorable truth, that once she surrendered to her husband, she would not even have that.

Rafe knew the moment she came outside that afternoon.

Not because he was glancing over toward the front door to the still-usable part of the manor far too often, though he suspected he might be, as galling as that was. He could feel it. Her. It was as if she changed the very air with her presence, made the spring breeze blow warmer, or made the clear air smell that much sweeter.

Or perhaps she simply inspires you to launch into dreadful poetry at the slightest provocation, he thought darkly. *Which should be appalling enough.*

But he turned anyway, and she was there.

He was supposed to be attending to the building supervisor's long-winded thoughts on why some of the walls in the burned out east wing were proving so tricky to put up, but instead he found himself watching his wife as she picked her way across the lawn, looking as delightfully out of place as she always did.

His wife. He let the words echo in him, liking them far more than he should. He couldn't understand why he found her so compelling. She stood out in every possible way—deliberately, he thought. She was wildly inappropriate, rather endearingly disrespectful, entirely too clever for her own good, and he was, he realized, quite shockingly fond of her.

He refused to allow himself to dwell on that. Or even to examine it in any detail.

The working men knew better than to ogle the countess in front of the earl, for which, today, Rafe felt some sympathy. She had yet to get the message that women of her new rank, in the country no less, did not dress as if they were taking a stroll through the high-end shops in some desperately fashionable part of London. Angel wore a pair of jeans that looked as if she'd glued them to her tight curves, a pair of completely unsuitable shoes and one of those immensely complicated, profoundly feminine tops that looked fussy and strappy and yet made him want nothing more than to take the whole thing off with his teeth. The high shoes made her hips sway invitingly—a sweet rhythm that made him even harder than he usually was, just at the thought of her—and there was something about her oversize sunglasses and deliberately mussed and choppy blonde hair that made him want to use his teeth in other places too.

She was driving him slowly insane. And the worst part was, on some level, he was actually enjoying it.

"I see you dressed to lend your hand to the ongoing construction," he drawled when she drew near. "How thoughtful."

"There are very few mirrors in this house," she replied, seemingly unbothered by his ironic tone. "I am forced to toss things together and hope for the best. You have only yourself to blame if you do not care for the result."

He had forgotten about the mirrors, he thought. He had the urge to look in one so rarely, he'd forgotten that he'd removed almost every last one of them from the house. Too many ghosts in the damned things, he'd found. He saw only the explosion and the terrible aftermath. He heard only the screams, not all of them his own.

"I hate mirrors," he said, realizing only after he spoke that his tone was clipped and dark.

"This outfit is meant to be my form of encouragement and support," Angel replied at once, merrily, smiling brightly at the building supervisor who reddened under the force of all that shine. As well he should, Rafe thought when she turned that same smile on him. It banished the dark, the ghosts. It made him want to lick her all over, as if she was made entirely of the sweetest, richest cream. "Are your spirits not lifted?"

"My spirits, certainly," he murmured in a low voice when the supervisor stepped away, out of earshot. "And many other parts of me."

"I'm sure I don't understand your meaning," she said demurely, with a quirk of her wicked mouth that indicated that, again, she was playing with him. *Playing.* With *him.* No matter how often she did it, it never failed to surprise him. He wondered why he found her so entertaining. He, who never found anything in the least bit entertaining, and hadn't, really, since he'd left Pembroke Manor as a broken, unwanted boy of sixteen to join the military academy that had made him a man.

"Put your hands on me the way we both know you want to," he suggested, not caring that he was standing out in public. That he was no doubt being watched, even now. She made him cease to care about everything except her— which should have given him pause. But it didn't. "The meaning will come to you, I'm sure."

But she only aimed that maddening smile at him, and then turned her attention to the clatter of the reconstruction going on in front of them. Rafe ordered himself to calm down, though he was starting to think that was well nigh impossible when in her presence. She slid her hands into the back pockets of those skintight jeans, which thrust her breasts forward against the delicate material of her top, and very nearly made him groan aloud.

"Is it going well?" she asked, utterly oblivious to the torture he was in. Or, perhaps, not quite as oblivious as she seemed, he thought, when she slid him a sideways look. He felt it like electricity, shuddering through him. Heaven help him, how he wanted her. "I'm afraid I can't tell. All I see is the scaffolding, and a whole host of tired-looking men stamping to and fro with very loud tools."

He bit back a smile, amazed, as usual, that one even attempted to appear.

"It is going well," he told her. "The loud tools are a good sign. You'll want to worry when it's silent out here."

He followed her gaze to the skeletal beginnings of the new east wing, the physical manifestation, he often thought, of his new beginning here. Of this new chapter in the history of the earldom and his dysfunctional family. One that might erase what had gone before—all those dark years he'd survived somehow while watching the rest of his family succumb to their demons, one after the other. One that had more to do with protecting and caring for the estates and all those who worked them, and less to do with bleeding those same estates for every penny, as Oliver had done with so much reckless entitlement. If it had not been for Rafe's stern discipline and careful stewardship of the relatively small inheritance he'd received from his father, and the personal holdings from his grandmother that she'd signed over to him before her death, Pembroke Manor might well have had to have been sold off. Chopped up into pieces, no doubt, and ruthlessly developed, like everything else in the whole of the United Kingdom these days.

He had not let that happen. He would not let that happen.

He would rebuild this house as a monument to the childhood he'd lost when his father died. To the boy he'd been so briefly back then. To what he might have been had he not become...*this*.

"Why do you love this place so much?" she asked, very much as if she could read his thoughts.

He should not have been surprised by another incisive question from her. He should have been used to it by now, surely. But he still found himself taken back, and frowned at the scaffolded ruin before him as if it would help him construct an answer.

"Do you mean that you do not?" he asked quietly. It wasn't a fair question, loaded as it was with all of his own personal history, and that of his family, stretching back through the generations. But he didn't rescind it.

"I can appreciate it, of course," she said. Carefully, he thought. He could not see her marvelous, expressive eyes behind those dark glasses, and he did not care for it—for being shut out. It occurred to him to worry at how completely he wanted her—how comprehensively—but he shoved it aside. "I can see that it is very beautiful, and very old, and I have the normal level of admiration for stately houses and historic estates." She shrugged, and tilted her head slightly as she regarded him. "But that is not what you feel, is it? For you, it goes much deeper."

"This is my home," he said simply. He crossed his arms over his chest because he wanted to put his hands on her, and that would not be wise, not out here in public. Not when he wanted it—her—far more than he should. "It was my father's pride and joy, and his father's before him, and so on, since the first small hall was built here sometime in the early fifteenth century. Though they say my branch of McFarlands have been living in this part of Scotland since the start of Scottish history, as far as anyone can tell. I want to honor all of that."

It was his form of penance, too, for having played his

part in the destruction of this place. For having contributed somehow to all that had gone on here. He could not help but think that if he'd been better, if he'd irritated his mother and brother less, perhaps none of this damage would have happened. He would never know. But he could rebuild.

"You never say you were happy here," she pointed out, something almost wistful in her voice then, reaching parts of him he'd thought he'd excised long ago, the parts that still remembered, with such clarity, those long, quiet walks in the woods with his father. The childhood he wanted so desperately to honor somehow. "You never mention any happy memories at all. Only duty and your heritage and other such things. Have you ever noticed that?"

"I will be happy when the manor is restored," he said after a moment, something large and unwieldy moving through him, despite his best efforts to clamp it back down.

"Will you?" she asked, and he could have sworn her voice was sad.

Temper cracked through him then. Or so he told himself. Temper was far easier to understand than this other thing that seemed to tie him up in knots, that forced him to feel any number of things he'd prefer to ignore completely. That he'd spent years ignoring, in fact.

"Do not waste your time making up sad stories about me to make me more palatable," he told her, far harsher, perhaps, than was necessary. "I keep telling you that this is no fairy tale, Angel. No kiss will turn me into Prince Charming."

"Clearly," she replied pointedly, without seeming the least perturbed by his tone, which only served to irritate him further. As did her light little laugh. "Maybe we should talk about your obsession with fairy tales then. You bring them up a lot. Do you read them nightly? Should I be careful when eating shiny red apples in this house?"

Rafe was well aware that he was picking a fight with her—that he wanted an explosion—and he even knew why. If tempers flared, so, too, would this repressed, contained passion that was making his life a misery. He wanted it to explode. He wanted it to incinerate them both. He wanted to force her to put her damned hands on him and rescue them both from this interminable waiting.

It was not the first time in his life he'd wished he was slightly less self-aware.

"Thank you for coming out here to offer your support, Angel," he gritted out, not sure who he was angrier with in that moment—her or him. Her, he decided, for being so constitutionally incapable of being properly scared off, properly cowed, properly *any* of the things she ought to be. Like being appalled at his monstrous appearance on that damned dance floor, so that none of this would have happened, and he could have simply rebuilt his house and marinated in his solitude, as planned. Without worrying that she would see the real ugliness within him. Without descending into sarcasm. "I'm sure it will speed along the restoration of the manor considerably."

She slid her sunglasses from her eyes, securing them on the top of her head and fixing him with her frank blue gaze. It was as if Pembroke Manor disappeared, with all of the workmen and the power tools, the stone walls the fire had failed to topple, the glittering loch and the silent sentries of the mountains in the distance. It was as if there was nothing at all in the whole of the world but Angel, and he was rapidly losing his ability to keep his cool where this woman, *his wife,* was concerned.

"Do not speak," he told her, his voice too dark, his patience too thin. "Unless you plan to invite me into your bed, right now. It is the only thing I want to hear from you at the moment."

Something he might have called fear in someone else moved through her bright eyes then, clouding them. Making her look soft for a moment. Vulnerable. Not the Angel he knew at all.

"I can't," she said, and laughed slightly, as if the admission surprised her. "I don't know why, but I can't."

His gaze bored into hers, daring her. Challenging her. He wished the power of his gaze alone could seduce her, somehow. Could make her want him enough to finally prove what she'd said to him that morning in the woods. Could make him believe that she truly saw all of him, and could accept it. Even if he knew better.

"What are you so afraid of?" he asked softly. Deliberately. "You already know I will make you come. Screaming my name, in fact."

Her breath came out in an audible rush that was, in part, a kind of dazed laugh. He did not try to hide the force of his desire, the sweet torture of it, and he had the satisfaction of watching her eyes widen as she shivered slightly, then the exquisite pain of watching her pull her lush lower lip between her teeth and bite at it. He felt it as if she'd bitten him instead. But once again that look moved over her face, and she shook it away.

"I have to go," she whispered, stepping back and breaking that odd enchantment that hovered between them and shut out the world. Rafe was aware, again, of the din around them, the crowd only a small distance away in the ruined wing of the house. He felt it as a loss.

She turned away. But her shoes were absurd and much too high for even the manicured sweep of lawn outside the manor, and she took only a step or two before she stumbled. Rafe didn't think, he simply reached over and righted her with a hand on her arm. And then, because he could, he acquiesced to an urge he hardly understood and swept her up and into his arms.

She clutched at his shoulders, her blue eyes wide, though she made no sound of protest. Holding her high against his chest, Rafe began to walk toward the house. She was light in his arms, a sweet weight against his chest, and he wanted her more than he had ever wanted anything. He could not seem to tear his gaze from hers as he shouldered his way through the great front door and into the grand entry hall. He was breathing too hard, as if he'd run up the side of one of the mountains, and he could only imagine the look that must have been stamped on his face. Arousal. Desire. As if he was some kind of wild animal, he thought in self-disgust, so desperate was he for her. And still she only stared back at him as if she was frozen in place, in his arms and in his gaze, as he carried her over his threshold.

The symbolism was not lost on him.

But this was a different sort of marriage, and she was a very different sort of wife, and he had no choice but to let her down from his arms. He did it slowly. So slowly. And if she slid a bit and rubbed against him on her way down, well, he could only do so much.

Her feet touched the ground and she took a shaky sort of step back, her eyes too wide, as if, finally, she was as frightened of him as she should have been from the start. Why should that surprise him so much?

"I will see you tonight," he said then, which was not at all what he wanted to say. Nor was he sure he could survive another meal with all of this tension and flame drawn so tight between them. He might just snap, spread her out on the antique table and take her as he longed to do.

He didn't know himself in that moment. His iron control seemed to have deserted him entirely. He could feel his hands clench as if they might simply reach for her, and his promises be damned—

But he could not be that man. He could not break his word. Not this time. He didn't know why it felt so important to him, but it was. He knew that it was.

"Maybe," he could not help but grit out, with passion and pain and something much deeper he refused to identify, "you will take the time to think more carefully about what it is you want, Angel. Because you continue to play with fire and it will burn us both."

He forced himself to turn, to leave her standing there, to make for the door. And when he heard her say his name he ignored it, because he wanted it too badly. He knew it couldn't be real.

"Rafe," she said again, her voice husky. And definitely not in his head. "Please."

He stopped walking, though he could not bring himself to turn around and face her again. He wasn't sure he could keep walking away from her. He wasn't sure he would, no matter his best intentions. No matter that it would be better for both of them if he did.

"I'm tired of these games," he said quietly, even bitterly. "I promised you I would wait, and I will. But—"

"I don't want to play games." Her voice was still shaky, but there was a certain note in it that seemed to hum in him, like some kind of tuning fork. He turned to look at her. Her pretty face was clear, her eyes a hot flash of blue, and all he could see was hunger. A hunger deep and wild, to match his own.

He hardly dared let himself believe it.

"What do you want?" he asked, his voice too quiet. As if he might startle her, and lose her, should he speak too loudly. "If not these endless games?"

Her eyes were so blue. Her face was so pretty, and

flushed now with the force of this thing between them, this great wilderness of desire. She blinked, and he thought he'd lost her, but she only raised her chin slightly, as if fighting off attackers he couldn't see, and met his gaze with that directness that he'd admired in her from the start.

"You," she said, and he could see the enormity of this move over her, through her, as if she felt it too, these impossible currents that flowed around them. That threatened to suck them both under, and Rafe couldn't even bring himself to care.

She stepped toward him, closing the distance between them. Rafe was not sure he breathed, and then he knew he did not when she reached over and put her hands on his chest, tilting her head back to gaze up at him, heating up the great hall until there was nothing at all but this shared hunger. This sweet fire.

Her. *Angel.*

"I want you," she said, her voice a mere scratch of sound. "I do."

And then she pushed herself up on her toes, closed the distance between them and kissed him.

CHAPTER NINE

FOR a moment he was still, too still, and Angel only pressed her mouth against the grim, sober line of his, as close as she'd ever come to begging. But it didn't feel like begging—it felt like some kind of homecoming.

And then everything seemed to burst into color and heat.

Rafe slid his hands into her hair, cradling her head between them even as he angled her mouth against his for a deeper, hotter fit. And just like that, he took control. He demanded. He possessed. He *took*. He tasted male and enticing and *Rafe,* and she could not seem to get enough. He kissed her as if they would both die if he stopped, and there was some part of her, Angel knew, that believed they would.

She didn't care where they were. Some small voice in her head whispered that they were standing in the entry hall, that anyone could walk in and see them—but she shoved it aside. Sensation bloomed into new sensation, and she soaked each one in. The devastating perfection of his mouth on hers. The strength and command in the hands that held her there, while his mouth plundered hers. That lean, hard body of his that was all around her now, right in front of her. Hers to touch. To taste. At last.

She couldn't seem to get close enough to him. Her clothes felt like impediments. Her breasts ached until she pressed them into the hard wall of his chest, and then they ached again, more, but in a way that made her whole body seem to hum. And melt. And glow.

"More," she demanded, wrenching her mouth from his.

He made a low noise in the back of his throat, some kind of growl, and then he simply picked her up again, as if she weighed nothing at all. As if there was nothing more natural in the world. His hands were warm on her bottom, holding her steady as she wrapped her legs around his waist, her absurd wedge heels falling from her feet with a dull sort of clatter against the floor. *He is so strong,* she thought, with a kind of sensual shudder as she imagined what he would look like naked, that powerful body stretched out above her. In her. Claiming her. Changing her. She couldn't help the small sigh of pleasure, of anticipation, that escaped her lips.

She was finally close to him. She was finally *touching* him. He started to move, carrying her up the formal stair, cursing under his breath when she leaned into him and started tasting the line of his jaw, then the sweep of scars across his ruined cheek. She felt him stiffen slightly, his breath leaving him in a rasp. He stopped moving, and turned his head, his mouth meeting hers, his kiss something approaching desperate. She met it. She exulted in it, and after a moment he began to move again.

It could have been moments or years, suspended in the sheer joy of touching him like this, but then he was striding into his rooms. The suite next to hers that she had never so much as glimpsed before now. Angel had only the vaguest impression of an immense space, heavy antique furniture and gold tapestries on the walls before he was tumbling her down in the center of his bed, a commanding affair all its own, and coming down on top of her.

Finally, Angel thought. Or, she thought when his eyes gleamed, perhaps she'd said it out loud.

He claimed her mouth again with that same devastating mastery, pressing her into the soft mattress. She welcomed it. He gave no quarter, shifting so that the hardest part of him was flush against the softest part of her, making them both inhale too sharply. Heat flared and rolled through her, making her feel like some kind of firework about to scatter across a dark sky. Angel felt that same heat at the back of her eyes, threatening to spill over, and she couldn't seem to worry about that the way she knew she should. She felt dizzy with the taste of him, shaky with the driving greed that made her want more, even now. *More.* More of his clever hands. More of his delicious weight over her. More of that impossible mouth against hers.

His hands were like fire, moving over her, making her burn and burn again. He pulled her top over her head with a quiet intensity that made her shiver in reaction. He cast it aside, his attention narrowing in on her breasts, displayed for him in a frothy pink concoction of satin and lace. His hard face pulled taut with desire, making an answering surge of heat wash over her. And then he dipped his head and pulled her nipple into his mouth, through the material of her bra, making her gasp and jolt against him.

She hardly noticed when he peeled the bra from her body too, but then his hot, wet mouth was on her breasts, teasing her and tormenting her, making her arch into him and writhe beneath him, making that knot inside of her grow hotter, tighter, harder. He shifted then, making short work of his own shirt and kicking off his shoes and trousers. But when Angel moved to do the same, he stopped her. He rose, gloriously, mouthwateringly naked, and moved to the edge of the bed.

Distantly, Angel was aware he said something. But she was transfixed, staring at his beautiful body as if she'd never seen a man before. Why did she feel as if that were true? He was all hard-packed, rangy muscle, and she hardly knew where to look. The wide, mesmerizing shoulders, all sculpted muscle and strength. There were matching scars scraped deep into his chest, but they only seemed to highlight his solid, devastatingly masculine physique. His arousal jutted out before him, and Angel felt that knot inside of her begin to unwind, turning into a thick, wet need.

She wanted to touch him everywhere. She wanted to learn his taste, his scent. She wanted him in ways that should have scared her.

"Let me," he said, perhaps not for the first time, and Angel thought her heart might explode in her chest when he knelt down before her and helped her shimmy out of her jeans. He pulled her thong from her hips with the same gentle ruthlessness, and then they were both naked. His dark gaze met hers, and Angel swallowed, suddenly as terrified as she was aroused. As if he could sense it, he slid his palms up the smooth length of her legs, making her breath catch in her throat, making the terror recede and leaving only that delectable, languorous heat in its wake. When he reached her hips his fingers curled around and then tugged her closer to him.

"Rafe," she began.

But he ignored her. He leaned forward and pressed his mouth to the core of her, licking his way into her molten center.

It was like dying, Angel thought, in the most glorious way possible—and then he shifted position and she stopped thinking altogether.

And Rafe set her on fire. Again and again and again. He used his lips, his tongue and even the faintest hint of his teeth. He used his hard, beautiful hands. And when she was gasping for breath, writhing helplessly before him, her mind completely and utterly empty of everything but this most divine torture, he pulled back.

Her hands were fists in the coverlet. Her legs were wrapped around his shoulders.

"The next time you say my name," he told her, his voice a dark sorcery that made her nipples draw tight in reaction, pure male satisfaction in every syllable, "I want you to scream it."

And when he licked into her soft heat again, she burst into a thousand pieces, and obeyed.

When she opened her eyes again, dazed and made new in ways she couldn't begin to contemplate, he was making his way up the length of her body, kissing a trail of fire from her hip bone to the underside of her breasts.

He moved over her, settling himself between her legs, and for a moment she could only look at him, feeling strangely fragile. Oddly vulnerable. And she could have sworn he knew it.

And then he moved against her. Teasing her.

The fire blazed anew, as if he hadn't just thrown her over the edge. It was hotter, wilder. She gasped as the inferno rolled through her, shocking her, her hands moving to grip his strong shoulders, her hips once again rising to meet him, as if her body was already entirely his. As he knew her own flesh better than she did, and could make her do his bidding that easily.

He moved again, a delicious, tempting slide of flesh against flesh, and she arched against him, all helpless fire and need, and she understood that, in fact, he could. He did.

Rafe met her gaze, his own hot and dark and some kind of wild silver, and then, impossibly, he smiled.

Angel felt her heart break.

And then he twisted his hips and drove deep inside of her.

He set a demanding rhythm, but Angel met it, her body

moving like silk against his, as if she'd been designed for precisely this. For this slide of skin, this unbearably shattering possession.

He slid his arms around her, pulling her even closer as his hips moved faster and faster, making that wildfire burn white-hot—and then Angel was falling apart again, falling into pieces, and this time he came with her.

They made love so many times that night and over the next few days that Angel lost track of time. Of the world. Of anything that wasn't Rafe or his mouthwateringly beautiful body, that she only wanted more the more she had him. Of the magical things he could do, again and again. It was as if they couldn't seem to quench the hunger, the need, no matter how many times they tried.

It was like being lost in a kind of fog, except Angel didn't care if she ever came out of it. He looked at her as if she was a wonder, as if she was perfect. He touched her as if he wanted nothing but to worship her. He was addictive, and he was her husband, and an odd feeling started to grow in her as each day passed and they explored each other more and more. It was buoyant, and ever-expanding. It seemed to resonate in his hard face when she looked at him, when she kissed him, making even that grim mouth seem softer, somehow. As if he felt it too.

She had the strangest suspicion it was hope.

Almost two weeks passed before she bothered to check her email again, to see how the world had got on without her. The answer was: perfectly well. She lay across her bed with her laptop and found herself having to struggle to come up with her usual flippant tone in the emails she exchanged with Allegra. As if all those tough outer layers she'd thought were a part of her had been scraped away now. Here. As if being with Rafe like this, as if theirs was the real marriage she hadn't known she'd wanted until it was too late, was making her...raw. She didn't know where to put that.

Not sure you want to hear this while you're off exploring the Scottish wilderness with your earl, Allegra emailed after several messages demanding more information about Rafe and her exact whereabouts, in response to that email Angel hardly remembered sending way back when. But I've had a visit from Chantelle. She gave me a rather large cheque (£15,000!) and said a lot of incomprehensible things about her bills. Please tell me that doesn't mean your bills? Please tell me she didn't...?

Oh, she did, Angel emailed in reply. And while £15,000 is a lovely gesture, that's really all it is—a gesture. The old Angel would have ripped Chantelle apart. She could have ranted on the topic of her mother's opportunism for days. It wasn't as if Allegra hadn't heard her vent about her mother before—especially in a situation like this. But this new version of Angel couldn't see the point. It wouldn't make her feel any better, and it wouldn't change things, so why bother?

It doesn't matter to me anymore, she wrote instead, feeling like someone else—someone far calmer and more at peace than she had ever been. As if being around someone as self-possessed and still as Rafe was somehow contagious. She found she liked this version of herself, with all her usual edges...softened. I'm sure she owes you at least that much. Keep it.

And what about poor Izzy? Allegra wrote back. No one's laid eyes on her since that scene at the engagement party. You're going to have to come back. It's all gone pearshaped without you in London, clearly!

Angel stared at that email for a long time. She was not, she realized with a trickle of something like shame through her belly, a particularly good sister to Izzy. She didn't even know what scene Allegra was talking about, having spent the engagement party completely engrossed in Rafe—though with Izzy, it could be anything, and had probably involved forcing herself into the spotlight in one way or another. It always did. Angel had always despaired of her half sister's antics, but for the first time it occurred to her to wonder if that was fair. Angel knew better than anyone how difficult it was to grow up with Chantelle as a mother.

Izzy is a survivor, she wrote back to Allegra. She'll land on her feet. It's the defining family trait. Say what you will about Chantelle (I mean that) but she always sorts things out in her favor, doesn't she? So will Izzy.

But she couldn't help thinking about her half sister long after she hit Send. It wasn't like Izzy to disappear from view for very long. She was much more like their mother in that regard—she'd never heard of keeping a low profile. But what did Angel know? She'd seemed to turn over a new leaf, quite by accident, in the wake of Allegra's engagement party. Why shouldn't Izzy?

"How is the outside world?" Rafe asked from the doorway, making Angel start. But she only smiled, letting her eyes drink in the sight of him, as if it had been years since she'd last seen him like this, all lean and dark and gorgeous, instead of an hour or two. Her stomach dropped in that now familiar little flip of reaction to him. And her body, so attuned to him now, readied itself for the pleasure he could deliver.

"Very much the same," she said, closing the lid of her laptop. She eyed him, standing there in the doorway, almost as if he wasn't entirely sure he wanted to enter the countess's chamber. She wondered, not for the first time, what kind of woman his mother had been. "The whole world is carrying on just fine without me."

Rafe prowled toward the bed. Angel felt her smile deepen.

"I am not," he said in a low voice when he was close.

He stood over her, his mouth slightly curved in that way she found toe-curlingly sexy. She wanted to taste it, him, and so she came up on her knees and moved to meet him. He took her mouth in a kiss so deep, so carnal, that she felt her whole body tighten and then burst into molten heat.

And that suddenly, she was desperate for him. Again.

Always, that little voice whispered inside of her, propped up by that brightness that seemed to glow more and more each time he touched her like this, each time they took each other higher.

And then his hands were on her body and she stopped thinking altogether.

He could not get enough of her.

Rafe kept waiting for the fever to pass, for the fire to subside, but it only grew worse. The more he had her, the more he wanted her. On the table in that dining room, just as he'd imagined. In the woods in the spot where she'd almost left him. In the gallery, beneath the austere frowns of his noble ancestors.

He was made of want. Of need. He knew every variation of her sighs now—what each one meant, how much pleasure each indicated, and what to do to ramp it up even further. He never tired of exploring her lovely body. He began to wonder if he ever would. He had always been the sort of man who concentrated on what was in front of him, but this was something more than simple focus. She distracted him even when she was nowhere in sight. She was like an itch beneath his skin, and all he could think to do was scratch it. Repeatedly.

He told himself that was enough.

Tonight he'd had to take a call during their usual meal time, and so looked for her in the library when he was done. As he expected, she was curled up in that same leather chair. And as usual, she was wearing one of her formal gowns, as she did every night, while he remained deliberately casual in response.

"You are dressed for a ball," he pointed out as he walked toward her. He realized he'd quickened his pace the moment he saw her, and didn't know where to put that. She set her book aside and watched him draw closer, a smile in her bright blue eyes if not on her lush little mouth.

"Who knows?" she asked. "Perhaps there will be dancing in Pembroke Manor tonight. Hope springs eternal."

He came to a stop in front of her chair and held out his hand. Her eyes widened, and he felt his mouth move in response. There was no getting around it—he was smiling. He felt it move through him like light.

What was it about her, he wondered, that made him believe she could cure the things in him he'd always believed were damaged beyond repair? Simply with that smile? Her touch?

"Dance with me," he said softly. Repeating what she'd said to him in the Palazzo Santina, he realized, with so much more between them now. Her answering smile told him she remembered it too. She slipped her hand into his and let him pull her to her feet.

She wore a gown the color of a good red wine, a deep, rich burgundy. It fell low on her neck, exposing her delicate collarbone, then framed her pert breasts with a line of draped ruffles from one shoulder before swirling down to her feet. The effect was somehow edgy and elegant all at once. She looked good enough to eat. She always did. She smelled of something soft and feminine, and her clever eyes glowed as they met his. He wanted to be deep inside her, moving, driving them both wild. He was hard and ready and even though he knew she would be ready for him too, he ignored the temptation and pulled her into his arms instead.

And they danced. Around and around the library, circling the old globe in its pride of place in the center. This time, they did not talk. They did not spar with each other. They only danced, as if they could both hear the same song, as if it played in them both, guiding their feet across the old, thick carpets. He held her in his arms as if she was his very own miracle come to life. *Perhaps she is,* some small voice whispered deep inside of him.

And then he spun her away, making her laugh in delight. He spun her back to him, dipping her down low in the sort of showy way that he would have abhorred in public. But this was for Angel. For that laughter of hers that made his chest feel tight. That made him believe. How he wanted to believe.

But when he pulled them both back to standing, he saw that she was crying.

"What is it?" He was shaken. "What's wrong? Are you hurt?"

Had the monster in him struck when he hadn't been paying attention?

"No," she said, laughing slightly, wiping at her eyes. "This is so… I never cry!"

"I told you I was a terrible dancer," he said softly, rubbing his hands down the seductive line of her back, wanting only to calm her. "I gave you fair warning."

Still, the tears fell, no matter how she tried to stop them, and Rafe found he could not take it, even if there appeared to be no particular crisis. He settled them both in the leather chair so that Angel was across his lap, and he tried to calm her the only way he knew how.

"It's not the dancing," she said through her tears. "It's not you. I'm not even sad!"

"Then what?" he asked quietly. But she didn't answer.

She cried, silent sobs shaking her as she sat against him, and Rafe found himself murmuring soothing words, laying kisses on the bare skin near her collarbone, tracing that enticing ridge with his tongue.

Slowly, her sobs eased. And then her breath came quicker. Rafe moved from her collarbone to her neck, and then he reached up to slide his hands into her short hair, loving the way she fit so perfectly in his palms. He angled her mouth to his, and kissed her. Slow, lazy. As if the fire that always blazed between them might dry her eyes. As if he could kiss her smile back to him.

He pulled back, and searched her face. Her eyes were still damp, but the storm had passed. He used his thumbs to wipe away the excess moisture beneath each of her eyes, and something seemed to swell between them. It was deeper than electricity, and somehow warmer than their usual fire. Rafe felt almost dazed.

"Rafe…" she whispered, and he kissed her again, feeling something too restless, too huge, move through him. He kissed his way from her mouth to her cheek and all over her pretty face, tasting salt and Angel. That thing between them seemed to hum and glow. Still, it grew, and when he pulled away again he was smiling like a fool, like the kind of person who smiled without reservation, and he couldn't even have said why.

"You shouldn't look at me like that," he said softly, searching her pretty face, marveling at the brightness there, and inside him, where nothing had been bright in a long, long time. "You don't know what I might do."

Because she looked at him with whole summers in her blue eyes, and her smile made him want to be the man she saw when she looked at him, whoever that might be. Whatever it took.

She reached over and pushed his hair back from his forehead with one hand. Her smile deepened, turned tender. She let out a sigh he couldn't categorize, and when she met his eyes again, they were bright with more tears.

"You can do anything you like," she said softly. "I love you."

And everything inside of him went cold.

CHAPTER TEN

ANGEL felt the chill immediately. He might as well have thrown open the window and let the cold night air into the room. Without saying a word, he shifted in the leather armchair beneath her and then stood, taking her with him to stand her on the floor and put distance she didn't want between them.

Angel only stood where he left her, numbly. She knew she shouldn't have said it. She didn't know why she had.

"What did you just say?" he asked, and she recognized that voice. It was so terribly remote. Distinctly unfriendly. It was the way he'd spoken to her when she'd first approached him in the Palazzo Santina. She looked, and his eyes were as frigid, as forbidding. He stood there like he was made of stone, dark and coldly furious, as inaccessible as if he wore a suit of armor instead of that old pair of jeans and long-sleeved shirt that clung to the hard planes of his beautiful chest like some kind of cruel taunt.

He was a stranger again. So quickly, so utterly changed. It made her heart hurt, and she wasn't at all sure what she could do to make it stop. To make *him* stop. She was afraid that if she looked down, she would see that they'd somehow ended up standing on the edge of some dramatic precipice, with nothing to do but fall. And fall.

"You know exactly what I said," she replied, unable

to make her voice light, but somehow keeping it even. "I didn't mean to say it, if that helps." She shrugged, feeling helpless and powerless and not at all sure how to combat that. "It just slipped out."

Like the tears. She wiped at her face, not knowing how to process the fact that she'd broken down like that, so completely, sobbing for the first time in all of her memory. So undone by the kindness in his gaze, the smile on his usually grim mouth, that she had only been able to weep in response. She didn't know how to feel about any of this.

But it was painfully obvious that he did.

"We have a very clear agreement," Rafe said, and something about his voice made her go very still. Too still. His eyes were frozen chips of gunmetal gray. His mouth was a flat line. "I am perfectly aware of what I purchased. You should be equally aware of what you sold."

She felt as if he'd kicked her. Hard and directly in the stomach. For a moment, she wasn't sure she could speak through the impact of it. It seemed to flare out, stealing her breath. She noticed her hands were shaking slightly when she went to smooth her skirt and she hated, suddenly, the fact that she was wearing a formal gown tonight. That here she was, playing dress up. Believing in magic and miracles. Giving in to *hope,* of all things.

She was furious with herself. And beneath that, something darker and far closer to despair turned over inside of her and started to grow.

"If you are going to call me a prostitute, Rafe," she said matter-of-factly, fighting to keep the pain from her voice, the shock and the fury, and all that swirling dark beneath, "just come out and say it. Don't hide behind vague euphemisms."

"You sold yourself for money," he said in that silky, insulting way of his. That dark eyebrow of his winged high, aristocratic censure of the first degree. She swallowed, and pretended she wasn't affected.

"Am I not allowed to love you?" she asked, her voice too quiet, but at least it did not quaver. At least, she thought, there were layers to this betrayal of herself. Degrees. "I don't recall signing anything that forbade it."

His face darkened and his eyes grew even colder. She wouldn't have thought it possible. She was torn between the urge to go to him and hold him, as if that might warm him somehow, and the urge to hide from this. From him. From her own limitless stupidity where this man was concerned.

"Do you think I don't know what's happening here?" he demanded. "I don't want this kind of act, Angel. I told you before."

"What kind of act do you think this is?" she asked, not sure she understood him. And not at all sure she wanted to. "What do you think I'm pretending?"

"I know what I signed up for, and it does not involve pretty tears and declarations of love," he said bluntly. Cruelly. "It won't work. Do you understand me? You can't manipulate me with emotional fantasies. *I bought you.* I never forget that and neither should you."

Every word was like a blow, all the worse after the sensual spell they'd been living in these past weeks, and Angel was so dizzy with the pain of it that she wondered for a panicked moment if she would topple over from the force of it all.

But she didn't.

One moment passed, then another, and still she stood there, reeling but upright. She didn't know if that was a good thing. Perhaps it would be better to fold—to give in. To let this particular storm pass over them and start again in the morning, when she could summon her usual airy manners and handle him the way she usually did. When she could make it all okay with a laugh and a smile.

But she couldn't seem to make herself look away. She couldn't quite bring herself to surrender. Not anymore. Not when so much was at stake. She'd had a glimpse of what they could have been, she and Rafe—and she wanted it.

Heaven help her, but she wanted it. She wanted all of him.

"I must have misunderstood," she said, still managing to keep her voice relatively even, as if what he'd said only rolled off her back. "I thought we entered into a mutually beneficial contract. A marriage."

"Yes, a marriage," he threw at her, his eyes so cold—the coldest she'd ever seen. She repressed a shiver. "And what a marriage it is. I am such a terrible creature that I was forced to buy myself a wife whose financial irresponsibility is what led her straight into my arms. What a joyous union indeed. How lucky we are."

"All this because I said I loved you," Angel said quietly. "It seems a little extreme, don't you think?"

"I don't want your love." His voice was like a lash. Angel had to fight to keep from flinching away from it.

He moved closer, so dark and big, looming there, and it crossed her mind that she should have been afraid of him—but she wasn't. It was almost sad, how much she wanted that to mean things it couldn't. It was even sadder how very much she wanted to simply reach over and wrap her arms around him. Even now.

"I want your compliance," he said, his voice a harsh whisper that might as well have been a shout. "I want your body. I want heirs. You can keep what you call love to yourself."

He turned then, and started across the sweep of Persian rug beneath their feet, as if for the door. As if, she realized in some mix of dawning horror and something else, something that rolled through her and made her stomach twist, he had said all he needed to say. And something in Angel snapped. She felt it break, hard, and then crumble into pieces.

She thought of his autocratic behavior the day of the wedding, and how hard she'd had to fight to keep from reacting as she'd wanted to react. She tried to imagine a lifetime of that—years upon years spent smiling when she wanted to scream. She wondered what it would be like when she was older, when she didn't have this body any longer, when she'd lost it to babies and gravity—when she was rendered wholly worthless to him. She thought about what it would mean to love this man like this, desperately and foolishly, and know that he would never, ever return it. Not if he could help it.

And she couldn't do it. Not now that she knew him so much better, so much more intimately. Not now that she'd seen him smile, heard him laugh, seen that there was more to him than all his grim seriousness, all his cold menace. She knew too much now. She knew *him*.

"No," she said. Her voice rang across the room, and she imagined she could feel it echo inside of her, like a church bell.

"This is not a debate," Rafe snapped in his arrogant way, turning back to fix her with that intimidating scowl. "It is not even a discussion."

"You can make all the pronouncements you want," she retorted. "It's not going to work."

"Our agreement—"

"I don't care." She shrugged when he stopped talking and stared at her as if she'd startled him. She felt a new kind of heat move through her then. It warmed her cheeks and was like electricity in her veins, crackling and snapping. *Temper. Finally.* "I know you feel things for me too. You can't just pretend it isn't happening because it doesn't fit into your narrow definition of what this is supposed to look like between us."

"What I feel for you is no more and no less than the basest form of lust," he threw at her with deadly accuracy. "And a great sense of relief that I was not required to waste my time pursuing you in the usual way, as I would have had to do if you were not so desperate nor so shameless. You are a convenience, Angel. Nothing more."

She told herself it didn't matter what he said now, that he was striking out deliberately. That it didn't have to hurt unless she let it. But she felt dizzy and a little bit sick, and she knew that was cold comfort, at best.

"I know that's not true." She hoped it wasn't true. She *hoped.* But she stood straight, though her hands were balled into fists at her sides, and looked him in the eye anyway. He stared back at her, so very grim, with that visible current of banked fury pulsing just beneath his cold surface. This, then, was that part of him he'd hinted at, that he'd indicated lived below his surface. But she didn't think he was quite as contained as he wanted to be. As he usually was.

There was a part of her that took that as a triumph.

"What is it you love then, Angel?" he asked, and she couldn't help but flinch slightly at the sound of his voice. It was like a blade. Whisper-soft and deadly, and it cut into her, deeper with every word. "Is it this face? I know exactly how beautiful it is—how entrancing. Or is it the monster beneath it, do you think? The one so terrible his own family loathed him since he was a child. Who somehow lived when all of his friends were blown to pieces all around him. Is it that you love? Or is it, instead, my endlessly attractive bank account?"

"Stop it," she hissed at him, hurting for him in ways that

made her hurt too. He moved toward her again, as if he couldn't help himself, his gait lacking his customary grace.

"What do you think, realistically, a man in my position would feel for the woman he *purchased?* The one who introduced herself to him in the first place by announcing that she was looking for a wealthy man to marry?" He slashed a hand through the air, a greater show of temper than she had ever seen from this watchful, still man, and it made her breath catch. "It could have been anyone at all unlucky enough to be in that ballroom. It happened to be me. You'll forgive me if *love* is not the word that springs to mind!"

She seemed to sway slightly on her feet, and there were bright spots of color high above her cheekbones, but she didn't back down. She didn't crumble. She squared her shoulders, drawing his attention, as ever, to her curvy little body displayed to such mouthwatering perfection in the wine-red gown.

But then, he thought cynically, that was her job, wasn't it? To be a constant enticement? Always desirable?

Her chin rose as if she heard him. As if she was ready to fight him, with her hands if necessary. He couldn't tell if he hated her for it or admired her misplaced courage. He only knew that he could not tolerate the din and clamor of the thunderstorm rolling around inside of him, and it was her fault. It was all her fault.

He'd known from the start that none of this was fair to her, but he'd wanted her. And now look what he'd done.

"You are such a coward, Rafe," she said after a moment, biting out the words as if she could not keep them in, and the thunder inside him turned liquid, hot and dangerous, and he felt nothing for a long moment but pure, scorching fury.

"Say that again, please," he invited her, not recognizing his own voice.

"A *coward,*" she repeated, enunciating each syllable, her chin titling up again in defiance. "I mean it."

"Of course I am," he retorted, letting out some harsh version of a laugh. That terrible heat pumped through him, making the control he had over his temper slip more than it should. He was too angry to yank it back again, and glared at her instead. "That is why I received the Victoria Cross. They hand out the highest medal in the land to the greatest coward, naturally."

If his sarcastic tone got to her, she didn't show it. If she was impressed at all by the great honor he'd so reluctantly received, she didn't show that either. Her blue eyes were darker than he'd ever seen them, and even through his anger, there was a part of him that hated that. That wanted the brightness back. That knew he was the reason it had disappeared.

"You hide away in this remote place, stamping about with a chip on your shoulder the size of the mountains across the loch," she said in a low, determined voice. "You *want* to be the monster in the room. You *want* to drown in your own self-pity. It lets you sit in your grand old house and brood about how miserable you are, without ever having to put that to the test."

"Because you, of course, never saw these scars, much less what lurks beneath them," he seethed at her, more sarcasm dripping from his frigid tone. "What a saint you must be, Angel, to be conveniently blind where so many others have been unable to see anything but. I'm sure that is a reflection of your goodness, and has nothing at all to do with how wealthy I am."

"I don't care about your money!" she cried, throwing

her hands out. "I don't care about any of this! I care about you—"

"Spare me the histrionics," he snapped. He had no memory of moving, and yet here he was, towering over her, so close he could smell the faintest hint of her delicate scent, and could see each ragged breath she took. His body knew only that it wanted her. That he wanted her. Even now. He should hate himself for that weakness. He knew he should. "As if I am likely to believe anything that comes out of your mouth. You can either do as I say, Angel, or you can leave. Those are your choices. This is not a relationship. You are not my lover. At best you're an employee."

"I believe you mean I am a brood mare," she supplied, her face gone white.

"So far, you are not even that," he said viciously. "You have cost me a great deal of money while giving absolutely nothing in return. I should be so lucky as to have a brood mare."

Her eyes darkened even further, and seemed to stand out much too starkly in her suddenly pale face, and Rafe knew he was the worst kind of bastard. But he couldn't seem to stop. The rage in him grew with every breath. The words she should not have said, the words he could never believe and never accept, reverberated in his head—getting louder every time, making him colder and colder with each rendition.

I love you.

Like a curse, those terrible words.

Everyone he'd ever loved was dead. And he was the only living common denominator. He knew what that meant. He'd always known.

"You're a liar," she whispered. "I was the one looking at your face tonight as we danced. I saw what you felt. Why are you so afraid to admit it?"

But he wasn't afraid, he thought, fighting back his anger, keeping all that ugliness inside. He was empty. Why couldn't she see that? He had been nothing but empty the whole of his life. The scars were a perfect reflection of what he was already—what he had always been.

"Rafe," she said urgently, making a crucial mistake and stepping closer to him, even putting her hand on his arm. He felt himself tense, but she didn't let go. "We can make this marriage whatever we want it to be. We can—"

"You forget yourself, Angel," he said coldly, bitterly, because she made him want to believe, damn her. Even now. "This is not an equal partnership. It is not a partnership at all."

"But it could be!" she cried, and for a moment he saw only the passion on her face, the wild determination in her darkened eyes. For a moment, he was almost swayed. And he wanted to be—he wanted it with an intensity that very nearly floored him. But then he remembered himself.

"To what end?" he asked, moving back so she had to either let go of him or be dragged along. Her hand fell to her side. "I told you what I want from you, Angel. You signed your agreement a thousand times. I don't know why we're still discussing it."

"Because I want more," she said, her voice slightly scratchy now, and nothing but misery in her gaze. Misery and that small gleam of battered hope that he recognized and knew was the most destructive of all. He wished he couldn't see it. It was too tempting. *She* was too tempting. "And I think you do too, somewhere in there. I know you do."

"You know nothing about me," he corrected her, softly, temper like a drumbeat in his head, his blood, beating out a harsh rhythm. "While I know entirely too much about you. What kind of partner do you think you could be, Angel?

You mounted up fifty thousand pounds' debt in all of two months' time. You live a hand-to-mouth existence, at best. You have no education, no polish, nothing at all but bravado. What do you have to offer?"

The library was silent then. He could not even hear her breathe. One hand crept to her collarbone, as if she held her pulse inside her neck. Or as if it hurt. Her gaze was wet, though no tears spilled over, and in a lifetime of hating himself, Rafe could not think of a moment he had hated himself more than this.

"Congratulations," she said in a thick voice. "I think you have finally managed to make me detest you."

"That matters about as much as love," he threw back at her. He laughed shortly when she shook her head. "If you don't like it, Angel, you know where the front door is. You've walked out before. I told you—you're always free to go. I won't do anything to stop you."

She stood so straight, so proud, with only her head slightly bent, as if that was all the grief she would allow herself to show. She pulled in a breath, as if to steady herself. He couldn't tell if he wanted to comfort her or if that was simply his own guilt, growing deeper by the second. He would allow neither one to influence him. She had to understand. She had to *see*. What kind of man he was, had always been. What kind of monster.

The moment dragged on, and still she did nothing more than stand there, as if he'd finally rendered her speechless. He told himself that was some kind of victory. He wanted to touch her. He wanted to reach out to her. He wanted to comfort her again, soothe her and hold her, and keep her from saying those terrible, destructive words. He wanted to go back to where they'd been before she'd said them. But look what his *wants* had done so far. He knew better than to trust the things he wanted. He knew better than to trust himself.

He turned away from her abruptly, making his way toward the door at the far end of the long room.

"I finally understand what you've been trying to tell me all along," she said from behind him. He didn't turn. He understood that if he did, he would not be able to turn away again. He was that weak.

"Good," he growled out. "It's about time."

He heard the rustle of her gown, and briefly squeezed his eyes shut as if that could fortify him as she walked to him and then drew up beside him. Her eyes were large, dark and haunted, and he regretted the things he'd said to her almost as much as he regretted succumbing to the urge to marry her in the first place. What had he expected? That he would cart her away to his little castle and make some kind of fairy tale out of this mercenary piece of business between them? Had he really been so stupid?

But she was Angel. She was so lovely. And she was so much more than that too. She *teased* him, as if there was nothing scary about him, nothing broken. And she looked at him as if he was simply a man. He didn't know how he could possibly have resisted her.

He only knew he should have.

"I understand that it is not the scars on your skin that cripple you," she said, facing him, looking more composed than he thought he would ever feel again. "It is this ugliness you carry around inside of you." She reached over and put her hand on his chest, her palm against the place where his heart should have been, and he jerked back, but she did not drop her arm. "You might as well have died with the rest of them, Rafe, because all you are now is one of your ghosts. Haunting this place, haunting yourself." She shook her head, a helpless look crossing her face. "You are poisoning yourself from the inside out."

He thought he said her name, but he made no sound.

And then she walked away from him, without a backward glance from those bruised blue eyes, and he lied and told himself it was exactly what he'd wanted.

She didn't think. She didn't have to. There was no staying here. There was no more *hoping*. If there was one thing she'd learned over the course of her life it was that when a man told you who he was, what he wanted and what he could give, it was the wise woman who believed him and governed herself accordingly.

And she was finished, finally, with being so foolish.

She grabbed a small bag from her closet and threw in the most basic things. A change of clothes. A few key toiletries. Her laptop and mobile.

She didn't sneak down the stairs or creep into the night. She walked into the kitchens, located Rafe's driver and asked to be taken into town. She didn't look back as the car took her down the long drive. She didn't do anything but stare straight ahead, telling herself she was fine. Over and over again. *Perfectly fine.*

Or anyway, she thought, fighting off that deep, dark well of despair that threatened to pull her under, she would be fine, wouldn't she? She had no other choice.

She would survive, she told herself as the car dropped her as directed in the sleepy little village that was the nearest thing to civilization in this remote bit of wilderness. *She would survive.*

She always did.

CHAPTER ELEVEN

HE FOUND himself in her room, long after he heard the car make its way down the drive toward somewhere, anywhere else.

It was funny that he thought of it as her room now, when it had always been the countess's room in his head before. As if he had been trying to distance her from the title. From him. Rafe did not doubt it.

He did not like that she'd left so many of her things behind. Most of them, in fact. That dark current of temper in him crackled to life, and he wondered, hotly, if she'd left the dress thrown across the bed and most of her clothes in the adjoining dressing room simply to taunt him with her absence. He wrenched the red wine-colored dress into his hand from the coverlet and then found himself lifting it to his nose, to catch the faint scent of her on the fabric. The temper subsided as quickly as it had come.

He knew it would all fade, in time. The scent. The memory. *Angel.*

He walked over to the large windows that looked out over the grounds of the estate, and from which he could see the new walls rising from the ruins of the burned-out east wing. Though it was dark outside, with no moon to light the way, he imagined he could still see the details of the ceiling joists that the workmen had just begun to lay over the top of the walls. It was coming together, just as he'd planned. Soon, Pembroke Manor would be whole again.

Rafe was increasingly less certain about himself.

He turned back around, unable to check a sigh, and looked across the elegant chamber to the large painting that dominated the far wall, staged to hang over one of the antique wardrobes that these days held linens. It was a formal portrait of a woman with long dark hair and deep, mysterious eyes, looking out from the canvas with a serious look on her elegant, oval face. She was, he supposed, an attractive woman. Perhaps even pretty. If he forced himself, he could look at the painting and see only the girl she must have been when it was commissioned—barely more than twenty, he thought. No hint of the future awaiting her in that calm gaze. No hint of the monster inside of her either.

"These walls are cluttered with your relatives," Angel had said at one point in that flippant way of hers that had made his mouth curve against the crown of her head. She had lain sprawled across his chest, her choppy hair standing in spikes he could not stop toying with, both of them a little bit dazed and replete in the aftermath of their passion. "It's like living in the center of a constant family reunion. How do you stand it?"

He'd been more interested in the enticing view of her exquisite bottom, naked and lush, than in the same old art on the walls. Especially in this particular room. He'd tested her curves with his hand, making her stretch luxuriously against him.

"I don't think I've paid attention to the paintings in this house in years," he'd said. "They are simply part of the Pembroke Manor legacy. They fade into the woodwork after a while."

But even as he'd said it, his gaze had moved across the countess's chamber to find the one painting that he'd never managed to either ignore or remove, much as he'd tried. Much as he'd told himself he wanted to.

"Who is she?" Angel had asked.

He'd wondered what Angel saw as she'd looked at the painting. Not what he saw, he'd been sure of that. Angel had no way of knowing the truth. There was no sign of who she really was in those painted features. He'd been surprised to find that there was some part of him that had wanted to lie about it—wanted to refuse to claim the relationship, as if that could erase the painful truth of it too. But for some reason, he hadn't lied.

"My mother," he'd said finally, when the moment had gone on too long. Angel had turned those clever blue eyes on him then, looking at him as if she could read him like one of the books she loved. As if, he'd thought in something closer to panic than he'd been comfortable with, she'd been able to see everything he'd shoved away inside, so far down he'd spent years pretending there was nothing there at all.

"You must have loved her very much," Angel had said quietly.

And he'd pulled her head down to his and kissed her, lazily and deliberately, stoking the fire between them, because the last thing he'd wanted to do was discuss his mother. Not with Angel, who, he'd suspected, would understand all too well the things he'd not wanted to say. Who would, he'd known, see all too clearly the great wealth of bitterness he carried inside, all these years later.

Now, alone, he stood before the same portrait and stared at it as if he was looking for clues. As if they would be buried there, in brushstrokes and oils. He saw the family resemblance. He shared her dark eyes, her high brows, the color of her hair. Oliver had had that same oval face and that same notoriously English peaches-and-cream complexion, while Rafe's distinctive bone structure and his

darker coloring were all from his father. Rafe had his father's height and leanly muscled build, while Oliver had
been shorter and stockier, just like her.

But more importantly than all of that, Oliver had shared
her alcoholism.

Nine years older than Rafe, Oliver had encouraged it,
participated in it and perpetuated it. Or maybe she had
been the one to encourage Oliver to join her on that long,
terrible path. What did it matter, when it all ended in the
same ignoble way?

"I wanted to love her," he said out loud, to the quiet
room, to the memory of Angel and her wicked half smile
as she'd moved to sit astride him, helping him forget. His
voice sounded raw. Harsh. "But I couldn't."

He felt a sort of wave crash over him then, catapulting
him straight into some kind of emotional undertow. He
couldn't breathe. He couldn't fight. He saw all those terrible images from his childhood cascade through his mind,
one after the next—all the jeering, the taunts, the vicious
insults. The long nights he'd spent huddled alone in his
grandfather's library, listening to that razor-edged merriment elsewhere in the house, hoping that *this time, this
night,* he would escape it unscathed. He saw himself, all of
fourteen, begging his brother not to drink with his mother,
and Oliver's sneering derision in return. He saw Oliver and
his mother huddled together in his father's old study, long
after the earl's death, swaying slightly as they drank their
poison and plotted. Always plotting. They'd fed off each
other. They'd made each other that much sicker, that much
nastier. And without the earl around to take them in hand,
they'd simply spiraled into that great darkness together.

By the time he'd left at sixteen, Rafe had been desperate
to escape. He'd hated them both equally and wholeheart-
edly. But never as much, and as totally, as they'd hated him.

As a grown man, he could look back and tell himself that it was Oliver's influence that had so eroded any hint of maternal affection—but he knew that wasn't entirely true. His mother was a woman who had fallen so head over heels in love with her firstborn child that there had been nothing left over, nothing left to share, nothing to give a second child. She should have stopped at one. But she hadn't.

She'd enjoyed his scars, he remembered now, the memories of his terrible initial recovery period after the explosion washing over him. He had been mourning so much—his friends, his face, the life he'd planned far away from his family—and she and Oliver had taken such pleasure in calling him those terrible names. *Quasimodo. Frankenstein's monster.* How they'd laughed! How they'd enjoyed their own sharp wit! He had been twenty-five and barely able to imagine life at all without the army, without his friends, much less with a ravaged, destroyed face.

They'd told him he was a monster. And he'd believed them.

He still believed them.

Rafe found himself moving before he knew what he meant to do. He reached up and jerked the painting in its heavy frame from the wall. Enough. He didn't have to look at her, and the parts of Oliver that came from her either. He didn't have to keep her hanging here, like a hair shirt, reminding him that the person who should have loved him most in the world had not managed to love him at all. *Enough.*

He moved to the fireplace on the opposite wall and he didn't let himself think. He cracked the painting over his knee, exulting in the loud sound it made as it broke in two. He should have done this years ago, he thought. And then he fed her to the fire. And watched her burn.

It was as if some kind of spell was broken. Something

hot and unbearably heavy moved through him, then, abruptly, was gone. His chest heaved as if he'd been running up the sides of the mountains outside. He thought of Angel's warm, sweet mouth as she'd explored each one of the scars on his face and across his torso, tracing them from start to finish, licking and kissing her way across them, until he suspected she knew them better than he did. Until he'd half believed that she had healed them with her touch alone, believed her capable of that. He thought of her first, arch comment on his disfigurement in that long-ago ballroom, her blue eyes sparkling with life, with merriment.

Not exactly the Phantom of the Opera, are you? she'd asked.

The manor house was so empty. He was so empty. Was that the McFarland family legacy? Would he molder away in this place? Both his mother and Oliver had died here, bitter and alone and incapacitatingly drunk. Was that his future too? Would he painstakingly reconstruct the manor house so it could stand as the perfect mausoleum to hold him as he slowly turned to dust?

He was already made of stone, he thought bitterly, staring at the painting as it blackened and curled. Who was to say he would even notice his own, slow decline?

You might as well have died, she'd told him, her blue eyes dark and haunted with the pain he'd caused her, *because all you are now is a ghost.*

And he understood then. It fell through him like light, like her smile, burning him alive from the inside out. Making him realize exactly what kind of life he was living here, and what it meant. What he would become if he continued along this path. If he continued to listen to the drunken jeers of the departed instead of the living, breathing woman who had dared to stand in front of him. And see him. She had truly seen him.

He could not repair the past; he could only restore the destroyed wing of a grand old house. He could not build his way back to a happy childhood or a loving mother. He could not make this house perfect enough to prove, somehow, to all of his lost family that he was worth the love they'd denied him.

He finally understood.

Rafe had been a ghost for most of his life, and Angel was the only person who had ever seen him. All of him.

And he had thrown her away.

It took most of the long night in a remarkably uncomfortable and frigidly cold village with a mystifying Gaelic name and then three separate trains to make it to Glasgow.

So far, Angel thought dully as she bought herself a much-needed coffee in the busy rush of the cavernous Glasgow central station, survival was not going particularly well. She had been cold and uncomfortable and *awake* for hours. Her return to civilization in the form of the Glasgow rush hour was overwhelming. She'd expected to feel safe, finally, away from all of that oppressive natural glory. She'd expected to feel right at home when she finally reached Glasgow. But instead, she missed the quiet of Pembroke Manor. She missed the desolate beauty of the loch and the far mountains. She missed the clear, fresh air in the cold mornings.

She missed *him*.

She took the first long sip of her coffee and almost burst into tears when the flavor flooded her mouth, stale and insipid in comparison to Rafe's personal family blend. She choked it down anyway, and was abruptly furious with herself. She'd lived for twenty-eight years without Rafe or his damned perfect coffee, and only a handful of months with him. She would get on just fine without both. She would.

Pull yourself together, Angel, she ordered herself sternly.
She jabbed impatiently at the eyes that were damper than
she felt they ought to be, and started across the vast concourse toward the immense Departures board to look for
the next train to London. She hadn't thought about what
she would do when she got there. There was time enough
on the train ride south to think it through, she reasoned.
She knew only that she had to get out of Scotland. She
had to put as much distance between them as possible. Up
above her, rain drummed down on the famous glass roof
that stretched for acres. She drained her coffee and then
set off for the appropriate platform.

She had the impression of him first, from a distance,
standing halfway down the platform—a tall, dark figure
dressed all in black in the center of the walkway, standing
perfectly still as hordes of commuters streamed around
him. Some of them did double takes to look more closely
at his face, his scars, and it took her longer than it should
have to accept the fact that it was Rafe standing there, grim
and quiet, waiting.

For her.

Her stomach dropped. And then flipped.

She should have turned and run. Anyone with any pride
would have done, but Angel couldn't seem to help the mas-
ochistic streak that ran through her and kept her walking
toward him. She wanted this to mean something, his being
here. She wanted things she knew better than to name. She
wanted him—still—to her great and abiding shame. But
this was Rafe, and she knew better than to hope. Look
where that had led her so far!

"Are you here to pick up your property?" she asked
coldly. "Your not-quite brood mare? Because I've quit that
position. You'll have to buy another one."

She came to a stop in front of him, rocking back on

her heels and tilting her head to look him in the eye. She couldn't read anything in all of that chilly gray. She didn't know what she thought she wanted to see. She shifted her bag on her shoulder, feeling something suddenly that was surprisingly close to shy. Awkward. A complicated rush of emotion worked through her, making her sway slightly on her feet. She told herself it was only exhaustion.

He reached over and traced what she knew were deep bags beneath her eyes, and his mouth tightened. She wanted to feel nothing when he touched her. She wanted to be blank—cured of that devastating addiction to him by the terrible things he'd said. But the same old fire danced to life low in her belly, filling her with chagrin. And need.

"I'm sorry," he said simply, devastatingly.

It was too much. She couldn't process it.

She felt her face crumple slightly, and she batted his hand away, fighting with herself until she got back under control. She felt unbalanced. Commuters jostled all around them, bursting with hurry and stress, but all she could focus on was Rafe, and the careening sensation inside of her. As if all of her screws were coming loose at once and she was in imminent danger of flying apart.

And then she felt nothing but the red-hot haze of rage. Everything he'd said, everything he'd done, flooded into her, and she was no longer frozen. She was no longer worried about losing him—she already had.

Which meant she had absolutely nothing left to lose at all.

"You can't just show up on a train platform and *apologize!*" she threw at him, her voice some kind of strangled whisper, the anger taking her voice away with its strength. "Do you think this erases everything? Do you think it *changes*—"

"Angel."

Just her name, in that dark magic tone of his. It shouldn't have affected her. She shouldn't have cared. All of the cruel things he'd thrown at her whirled in a loop in her head, and the misery of it, of this, threatened to swamp her. She should hate him. She hated that she didn't, that she couldn't, and she focused it all on him.

"It was my mother, by the way," she told him, tears in the back of her throat, distorting her voice. He blinked. "My mother is the one who ran up that bill. She used my name to get the credit card. It was her debt—but I knew she wouldn't pay it. She doesn't have the money and even if she did, she has convenient amnesia when it comes to her debts. What was I meant to do?"

"I believe you," he said quietly. "I do."

"Did I deserve those things you said to me?" she demanded wildly. "Did I deserve the names you called me?" He moved as if to put his hands on her upper arms, as if that might soothe her, but she twisted away. "Don't!" she said sharply. "That won't work anymore."

She worried it would work all too well.

"Listen to me," he said, and that was the Rafe she knew, autocratic and demanding, his hard mouth set in that granite line. She told herself it only made her angrier.

"I don't want to listen to you," she retorted. "I've done nothing but listen to you for months. You can listen to me for a change. I'm going back to London. I don't want anything to do with you. I don't even want your money. I don't know how I'll pay off that fifty thousand pounds, but I'll manage it." Her mouth twisted. "After all, as you so kindly pointed out, there's always money in prostitution, isn't there?"

He didn't answer, as the train that had been sitting next to them on the track lurched into motion and started rolling out of the station. Angel stared at it, anger pounding in her veins, too close to tears again and far too off-balance. The train leaving was the last straw, somehow, even though some part of her knew that there would be another one. There always was.

But she wanted away from him. From the whole of Scotland. From manor houses in the wilderness and Georgian townhomes in the heart of London, countesses and earls and weeks of insulting contracts. From these past months of her life, this crazy idea that should never have been made real—this marriage. She wanted to pretend that none of this had ever happened. That it hadn't touched her. That she was perfectly, happily whole.

She wanted to be on that train.

"This is pointless," she muttered, turning on her heel and heading back toward the concourse. She had no particular destination in mind, she just wanted to get away from him, so she could clear her head. So she could *think*.

"I love you," he said.

He didn't shout it. He simply said it, and still it slammed into her like bullets. *One, two, three.* Angel jerked to a halt, dimly aware that she was lucky the platform was now empty. There was no one left to watch her bleed.

Her heart pounded. Hard and then harder. Something ugly and powerful rolled through her, nearly flattening her, too big for her to contain. Too much to tamp down, to hide. She turned around to look at him. Those cold eyes, that dark, ruined face. How she loved him, to her detriment.

And she would never forgive him for this. Never.

"You would say anything, wouldn't you?" she threw at him, her voice shaking. Rage and pain, mixed into something toxic. She thought she might be crying again when he started to blur in front of her, and she no longer cared. "You would tell any lie you had to tell. You don't care about anything except that house of yours, and the heirs you want to fill it with. You couldn't love me if your life depended on it. You wouldn't know where to start."

"And what if my life does depend on it?" His voice was urgent, and there was something in that gray gaze—but she couldn't fall for that anymore. She couldn't let herself care. "I think it does."

"Do you have any idea how hard it was for me to tell you I loved you in the first place?" she demanded. "I cried, Rafe—and I never cry. The one thing I always promised myself was that I'd never fall in love, that I'd never give someone that much power over me—"

"Angel," he said in a low voice that seemed to reach into her, finding her most vulnerable places and wrapping around them and demand, "don't you understand? All I've ever had are those ghosts, that poison. You terrify me too."

She didn't want to understand. She wanted to disappear. She wanted things to be easy again. She wanted to be anywhere but in the middle of all this painful truth telling. Anywhere but near this man, the only person alive who had ever seen her like this. No mask. No pretty words. Not even showing off her body to distract him. Nothing at all but Angel.

She couldn't take it.

"Go to hell," she raged at him, and then she turned around again, mindless and panicked, and simply ran. She dropped her bag at some point, and she didn't care. She dodged through the crowds in the concourse, weaving her way around them, running as if it was her life that depended on it now. She knew without a doubt that it did, and she didn't even know why.

She burst through the grand doors of the station and out into the street. Only then, in the pouring rain, did she come to a stop. She simply stood there and let the rain fall all over her, soaking her, while she gasped for breath. And somehow she was not at all surprised to find Rafe standing next to her, holding her bag, not even breathing hard.

"Run wherever you like," he said, his voice tight, his eyes intense. "As long as you feel you must. It doesn't matter. I will always find you."

"As if you'd want to find me!" she tossed at him, incredulous. And something else beneath it, something she ignored. "Why don't you find someone else?"

"I want *you*," he said. Implacable. Sure. "I married *you*."

"I can't do this," she said, tears mixing with the rain, and she couldn't bring herself to care. "I can't live like this. I never should have approached you—"

"But you did," he said, some fierce note in his voice that she didn't fully understand, though her body heard it and warmed. "And here we are."

"It's your fault!" she accused him. "It was just a crazy idea. I never would have gone through with it! But you were so…" She shook her head, wishing she could clear it, but nothing seemed to work. Not since the day she'd met him, if she was honest. "I never really meant for any of this to happen."

"While I can't regret a single moment of it," he said. He shifted, this strong, powerful man, as if he was uncertain. As if she meant that much to him. But how could she believe that? He sighed, slightly. "I don't want to be a ghost anymore."

She turned toward him, searching his face, looking for something she wasn't even sure she would recognize if she found it. That great red rage left her in a sudden rush, along with that driving, instinctive need to run, and she wasn't at all certain what was left. But she couldn't seem to look away from him as the rain came down in sheets all around them, over them.

"I have been alone all my life," he said gruffly. "I lost

my father too young. My mother and brother excelled at cruelty. They enjoyed it. The only friends I ever truly had were in the army, and they all died in that explosion." His mouth tightened, and shadows twisted through his dark eyes. "I survived, but I was covered in scars. Suddenly my outsides matched what I'd always thought was already on the inside." He looked away for a moment, as if he was battling something, and then met her gaze again, his own fiercely probing. Furious—but not, Angel understood, *at her*. Perhaps none of this had ever been aimed at her. "My mother only told me she loved me when she was playing one of her games," he said softly. "She thought it was funny if she could get me to believe her, even for a moment."

"Rafe…" she whispered, her throat tight, her heart seeming to somersault behind her ribs. Something in her shifted then. The fear fell away, the hurt seemed to subside, and all that was left was that same old feeling, that sharp urge to protect him, somehow, even from this, his own past.

Maybe she had loved him all along.

"You are the first person I've ever known who is more beautiful inside than out," he said, his eyes so dark, so very dark, and Angel felt it inside of her. "I don't know why you love me," he continued in the same low voice, twisting in and around the rain that fell upon them, and her heart began to pound. "I don't know if I've already ruined it. All I've ever seen in me are these scars, long before they showed on my face. Ugly, incapacitating scars, in and out, that make me wholly unfit for the company of others. I don't know why you approached me, and I can't think of a single reason why you would stay."

She couldn't speak. He raised his hand, cautiously, and when she didn't flinch away, he slid it over her jaw to cup her cheek, leaning down close, as if the rain that fell on them was some kind of blessing. As if it held them there, in a kind of embrace, cocooning them. Washing away all the harsh words, all the pain. The past. Their families. All their shields and armor, masks and hiding places.

Clearing the way, somehow, for whatever came next. Making space for their strange marriage, their rocky start. Making it feel new. Right, somehow.

"What I know is that you are like sunlight to me," he said, his voice ragged, but sure, and his eyes warming to quicksilver as he looked at her. "You make me want to come out of the dark, Angel. You make me want to believe that I can."

She felt that dangerous spark of hope ignite within her, but this time, she let it glow. She felt it turn into a fire, then grow into a blaze. And then it began to spread. And spread.

And she let it.

"You can," she whispered, almost overcome with the heat of all that hope.

She was lost again, but this time with him. In him. Where she belonged. Where she would stay. No masks. No scars. Just them. She smiled then, a real smile, and after a moment he returned it.

"I am skeptical," he whispered, and she could hear the pain in his voice, the monster he believed himself to be, the fear. It made her heart ache. She concentrated instead on the matching gleam of hope she could see in his dark gray gaze, and she knew, somehow, that it would be okay.

That they would make this work, make it real. Together.

"I am not," she said. She turned her face into his palm, and kissed his hand. Loving him, pure and simple. Forever. She smiled wider. "I'll show you."

* * * * *

COMING NEXT MONTH from Harlequin Presents® EXTRA

AVAILABLE SEPTEMBER 4, 2012

#213 GIANNI'S PRIDE

Protecting His Legacy

Kim Lawrence

Can Gianni conquer his pride and admit that he might have met his match in utterly gorgeous Miranda?

#214 THE SECRET SINCLAIR

Protecting His Legacy

Cathy Williams

One spectacular night under Raoul's skilful touch leads to consequences Sarah could never have imagined: she's pregnant with the Sinclair heir!

#215 WHAT HAPPENS IN VEGAS...

Inconveniently Wed!

Kimberly Lang

Evie's scandalous baby bombshell will provide tantalising gossip-column fodder, unless she marries the dangerously attractive billionaire Nick Rocco...father of her baby!

#216 MARRYING THE ENEMY

Inconveniently Wed!

Nicola Marsh

Ruby finds herself propositioning tycoon Jax Maroney in order to save her family's company—but it's only a marriage on paper...isn't it?

You can find more information on upcoming Harlequin®
titles, free excerpts and more at www.Harlequin.com.

HPECNM0812

REQUEST YOUR FREE BOOKS!

Harlequin *Presents*

2 FREE NOVELS PLUS 2 FREE GIFTS!

PASSION GUARANTEED SEDUCTION

YES! Please send me 2 FREE Harlequin Presents® novels and my 2 FREE gifts (gifts are worth about $10). After receiving them, if I don't wish to receive any more books, I can return the shipping statement marked "cancel." If I don't cancel, I will receive 6 brand-new novels every month and be billed just $4.30 per book in the U.S. or $4.99 per book in Canada. That's a saving of at least 14% off the cover price! It's quite a bargain! Shipping and handling is just 50¢ per book in the U.S. and 75¢ per book in Canada.* I understand that accepting the 2 free books and gifts places me under no obligation to buy anything. I can always return a shipment and cancel at any time. Even if I never buy another book, the two free books and gifts are mine to keep forever.

106/306 HDN FERQ

Name _____ (PLEASE PRINT)

Address _____ Apt. #

City _____ State/Prov. _____ Zip/Postal Code

Signature (if under 18, a parent or guardian must sign)

Mail to the **Reader Service:**
IN U.S.A.: P.O. Box 1867, Buffalo, NY 14240-1867
IN CANADA: P.O. Box 609, Fort Erie, Ontario L2A 5X3

Not valid for current subscribers to Harlequin Presents books.

Are you a current subscriber to Harlequin Presents books and want to receive the larger-print edition? Call 1-800-873-8635 or visit www.ReaderService.com.

* Terms and prices subject to change without notice. Prices do not include applicable taxes. Sales tax applicable in N.Y. Canadian residents will be charged applicable taxes. Offer not valid in Quebec. This offer is limited to one order per household. All orders subject to credit approval. Credit or debit balances in a customer's account(s) may be offset by any other outstanding balance owed by or to the customer. Please allow 4 to 6 weeks for delivery. Offer available while quantities last.

Your Privacy—The Reader Service is committed to protecting your privacy. Our Privacy Policy is available online at www.ReaderService.com or upon request from the Reader Service.

We make a portion of our mailing list available to reputable third parties that offer products we believe may interest you. If you prefer that we not exchange your name with third parties, or if you wish to clarify or modify your communication preferences, please visit us at www.ReaderService.com/consumerchoice or write to us at Reader Service Preference Service, P.O. Box 9062, Buffalo, NY 14269. Include your complete name and address.

HP11B

Second in line to the throne, Matteo Santina knows a thing or two about keeping his cool under pressure...until he meets pop star Izzy Jackson

Enjoy an exclusive excerpt from the next book in THE SANTINA CROWN *miniseries!*

DEFYING THE PRINCE
by Sarah Morgan

***

"I WOULD curtsey but honestly these shoes are completely killing me so right now I'm trying not to move. If you were a girl, you'd understand."

He growled deep in his throat. "You are the most frivolous, pointless woman I've ever met. Your behavior is appalling and the damage that someone like you could do to the reputation of my family is monumental."

Izzy, who had been called many things in her life but never "pointless," was deeply hurt but at the same time oddly grateful because surely she could never truly fall for a man who was so horribly insulting.

"I happen to think it's *your* behavior that's appalling. Why is it good behavior to make someone feel small and inferior? You think you're better than me, but if someone comes into my house, I smile at them and make them feel welcome, whereas you look down on everyone. I've had more impressive hospitality in a burger bar. You may be a prince and actually far too sexy for your own good, but you don't know anything about manners." Lifting her nose in the air she was about to say something else when the door opened and a white-faced member of the palace staff stood there.

"The microphone, Your Royal Highness," he said in a strangled voice, addressing himself to the stony-faced prince. "It's still switched on. Everything you're saying can be heard in the ballroom. On high volume."

***

DEFYING THE PRINCE
by Sarah Morgan

Available in September 2012
from Harlequin Presents®.